D0896291

*A*
*Harlequin*
*Romance*

OTHER
*Harlequin Romances*
by ROZELLA LAKE

1862—CHATEAU IN PROVENCE

# IF DREAMS
# CAME TRUE

by

ROZELLA LAKE

HARLEQUIN BOOKS    TORONTO
WINNIPEG

Original hard cover edition published in 1974
by Mills & Boon Limited. This book was originally
published as written by Roberta Leigh.

© Scribe Associates 1974

SBN 373-01893-2

Harlequin edition published July 1975

Printed in Canada

1893

# CHAPTER ONE

BRIONY STEVENS paused with her hand on the latch of the door and turned to look at her sister. Even from a distance she was struck by Fay's heightened colour and the lines of pain that creased the high forehead.

"I hate leaving you alone," she said. "I'll telephone and see if Tom can come over and look at you."

"I've only got a headache," Fay remonstrated. "I always get it when I work with seed pearls."

"You should tell Mr. Van der Heim. He always gives you the most difficult jewellery to repair."

"Because I'm his best worker." Fay's expression was half wry, half proud. "It's my only claim to fame. What else can a cripple like me do!"

"Don't!" Briony ran over and caught her sister by the shoulder, wishing desperately that Fay would accept her lameness without pretending to a strength she did not have; a strength which invariably let her down in moments of tension. As it was doing now – when she was keyed up at the prospect of the ordeal ahead of Briony.

"Stop working on the necklace and go to bed," she pleaded.

"I will, if you'll stop fussing. Now go to the theatre or you'll be late."

Briony pulled a face. "What's one swan more or less? If I call Madame Cassini and say you're ill, she'll put –"

"I won't let you call anyone," Fay said firmly. "This is your first really big solo and I'm not having you miss it because of me. Now go!"

Knowing that unless she did Fay could well have hysterics, Briony hurried from the flat. But once in the street she headed

5

for a telephone kiosk and dialled Tom Bristow's number, hoping he was still in surgery; if not, she would call the theatre and say she could not appear. It might put paid to her being asked to dance a solo again, but she had no choice. She was too worried about Fay to leave her alone all evening.

The telephone receiver at the other end was picked up and she hurriedly inserted a coin.

"Briony!" There was no doubting Tom's pleasure as he recognised her voice. "I was just thinking about you and wishing I could see you dance tonight. But unfortunately I'm on call."

"I know you are. That's why I'm ringing. Fay isn't well," she explained. "She's working herself up to one of her attacks."

"I'll be over as soon as surgery's finished. I'll get my calls switched through to your flat, and stay with her for the evening."

"You're an angel," Briony exclaimed. "I don't know what I'd do without you."

"Find another doctor who'd do the same," he chuckled. "Men are push-overs for willowy young ballet dancers!"

Feeling a burden had been lifted from her shoulders, Briony went to the theatre. She and Fay had known Tom when he was a gangling medical student and they had been two starry-eyed schoolgirls begging to see the skeleton he had kept in his study. How happy those days seemed in retrospect. Because there had been no money worries, Fay's lameness had not assumed the importance it had now. Only after their parents' death, when shortage of money had brought them to an old-fashioned flat in a dreary neighbourhood, had Fay's illness grown worse, with bouts of depression increasing her lameness and continuing lameness adding to her depression.

Briony had been on the edge of a breakdown herself when, leaving the theatre one night, she had found Tom Bristow waiting for her at the stage door.

It was the first time she had seen him for three years. He had been working as a houseman in a provincial hospital when her parents had been killed in a car crash and by the time he had returned home she and Fay had long since left the neighbourhood, unwilling for anyone to know how improvident her parents had been – indeed after their debts had been cleared there had only been sufficient money to pay for their flat and Briony's final years of training as a ballet dancer, a training she would have given up had not Fay insisted she continue with it.

"Dancing is all you care about," Fay had cried. "I won't let you give it up because of me."

"It isn't because of you," Briony had protested.

"But you wouldn't give it up if I were a normal person?"

"You're not abnormal just because you limp!"

"Limp?" Fay had laughed bitterly. "I drag one leg behind me like a lame rabbit. But that's why *you've* got to be a dancer. It means as much to me as it does to you."

In this respect Fay had spoken the truth, for as the years passed she seemed to live for her sister's success. And how slow that success was in coming! Long years of arduous training were followed by equally arduous years in the corps de ballet, and this gradually resulted in small solo parts when they were on tour and finally the occasional solo when they were in London.

It was seeing Briony's name in the programme a year ago that had brought Tom Bristow round to the stage door. Qualified as a doctor, he now had his practice in the neighbourhood where Briony and Fay lived. He saw the coincidence as fate – the same fate that had made him go to the ballet and see Briony's name. From then on he had made himself available as a shoulder to lean on: not only as a doctor but also as a friend.

Knowing he would be with Fay now gave Briony the peace of mind to go to the theatre and dance, though it was not until she was actually on stage that the magic of the music finally obliterated her worry.

"Not bad," said Madame Cassini, the dancing mistress, as she came off stage, panting heavily and sweating. "Too fast at the end, but not bad."

In Madame Cassini's terms "not bad" was high praise, and with a light heart Briony went to the dressing-room to change into her street clothes. With the tutu discarded, worry for Fay returned, and not waiting to remove her make-up she left the theatre.

Only as she reached the dingy block of flats and saw Tom's car parked by the kerb did she breathe a sigh of relief. At least Fay had not been left alone. Racing upstairs, she unlocked the front door, and was in the living room before she saw there was a third person there: a tall young man with sun-blond hair and bronze skin.

Tom rose to greet her. Short and stocky, he already looked the epitome of the family doctor, with a good-natured face, brown eyes with an unfailing twinkle in them and brown hair that never looked tidy no matter how often he combed it.

"How did it go?" he asked, putting an affectionate arm on hers.

"Madame Cassini said it wasn't bad."

"That means Briony was wonderful," Fay said.

Her cheeks were still flushed, but the hard brightness had gone from her eyes. Whether this was due to Tom's presence or the sedative he had given her, Briony did not know. All she knew was the ineffable peace of being able to relax. It was at times like these that she realised the heavy burden of being responsible for someone else's well-being. If only something positive could be done to help her sister instead of the continual tranquillisers and pain-killers.

"I hope you don't mind my asking a friend to join us?" Tom interrupted her thoughts. "When I promised to keep Fay company I'd forgotten I'd made arrangements to see Chris."

He waved his arm in the direction of the elegant young man who had risen to his feet and was regarding Briony with interest. "Christopher Clayton," he added. "We were at Cambridge together but lost touch when I went to medical school."

"We wouldn't have lost touch if I'd known you mixed in such glamorous circles," Christopher Clayton replied, and though he incorporated Fay in his remark, his eyes rested on Briony, making her aware of her shabby black dress and her hair still pulled starkly back from her face. She was unaware that the simplicity of her appearance – at variance with her theatrical make-up – made her a particularly arresting figure, or that the simple dress accentuated the fine-boned delicacy of her body.

"With such a gift for blarney," she smiled, "you must be Irish!"

"I don't believe in blarney," he laughed. "What I've just said is true."

"Compliments won't feed a starving woman," Tom intervened. "Fay and I made a casserole for you, Briony. It's warming in the oven."

"I'm not hungry," she protested.

"Briony eats like a bird," Fay complained. "She worries so much about me she never thinks of herself."

"You know the answer to that, funny face," Tom said. "You must try and get better."

"I'm not going into hospital for any more examinations, if that's what you're suggesting."

"I think I'll have the casserole after all," Briony murmured, and went into the kitchen.

Steps followed, and as she bent to the oven Christopher Clayton came in and watched as she served herself.

"You *do* have a bird's appetite," he smiled.

"I'm never hungry when I'm worried."

"About your sister, you mean?" He straddled a chair. "What's wrong with her? It's more than lameness, isn't it?"

9

"She gets attacks of hysteria. Tom's given her pills, but she won't take them. She says they make her walk more badly."

"That's nonsense."

"I know, but it's hard to argue with her. She's very self-willed."

"I rather got that impression." He leaned his arms on the back of the chair. The bright electric light shining directly down on to his head could find no flaw in his Nordic good looks. His thick blond hair was combed casually back from a high forehead, and long fair eyelashes marked clear hazel eyes. Though slim, he had the air of a Viking, and certainly the same air of lordly assurance as he gazed at her.

Uncomfortably aware of his gaze, she said: "Are you a doctor, too?"

"Good heavens, no! The thought of blood turns my stomach! I'm an architect."

She eyed his elegantly cut grey suit. "You look a successful one."

"I manage," he said easily. "It's the sort of profession where whom you know can be as advantageous as what you know."

"Is that why you chose it?"

"Miaow!"

"I'm sorry," she said quickly. "I didn't mean to be catty."

He smiled. "What you said is true, though. But it doesn't only apply to architecture. You get it in medicine too. Not with your general practitioner, but among specialists and in hospitals. . . You can't beat influence." The blond head tilted. "I'd have thought it particularly applied in the entertainment world!"

"You've been reading too many Sunday papers!" Her laugh was husky and the look on his face showed her he appreciated it. "Ballet isn't that sort of profession," she went on. "You can't hide lack of talent behind a beautiful face or a sexy

10

body! Either you're a good dancer or you're not. And if you're no good, you won't succeed."

"Will *you* succeed?"

"You need luck too," she parried.

"Luck for what?" Tom asked from the doorway.

"For success," his friend said, and took a gold cigarette case from his pocket.

"You're certainly a success," Tom grinned.

"You could be too if you set up in the West End instead of the Harrow Road!"

"Sick people are sick no matter where they live," Tom said briefly.

"That's my point. So you might as well take care of the rich ones! At least you know they'll take care of you!"

Tom looked at Briony and shrugged. "Now you know why I don't see much of Christopher. Too long in his company and I'd end up a dissatisfied doctor!" He held open the door. "Go and charm Fay, will you, Chris? I'd like a word with Briony."

One blond eyebrow raised. "Do I smell a romance?"

"No such luck," said Tom. "I'm strictly the family doctor and faithful friend."

"Good," Christopher replied, staring at Briony. "I like to know where I stand."

The door closed behind him and Briony looked at Tom, too anxious about Fay to think of herself. "She's getting worse, isn't she?"

"I think so. I'm sure there's something physical causing her outbursts. It's more than just nerves."

"She's been X-rayed so many times, and they still can't find anything."

"Techniques are improving all the time, and they've a new one that —"

"I daren't ask her to go for another examination. When she came out of hospital two years ago she said she'd kill herself rather than go back again."

11

"She didn't mean it."

"I'm not so sure. You don't know what she can be like sometimes."

"I do," he said softly, and came to stand beside her. "I wish you'd let me take the burden from you. If only you'd marry me."

"I don't love you, Tom, and I don't think you love *me*."

"If you mean I don't try and make love to you whenever we're alone. . . ." He sighed. "I force myself not to."

"And you succeed because you don't love me," she insisted. "One day you'll agree with me."

The telephone rang and he gave an exclamation. "That can only be for me at this hour," he said, and hurried to answer it.

When Briony came into the sitting room he was putting down the receiver.

"Mrs. Jalpardi's sixth baby has decided to arrive a month early. I'd better push off in case it arrives before I do!"

"Will you come and see me tomorrow?" Fay asked.

"If I can." He tweaked her long straight hair which she wore in an Alice in Wonderland style, held back from her thin face by a tortoiseshell band. "But I stand in for another doctor on a Thursday and I mightn't have the time."

"I'd better push off too," Christopher Clayton said. "You girls must be tired."

Briony glanced at the delicate Sèvres clock on the mantelshelf – one of the few pieces she had managed to save from the family home – and saw it was one o'clock. No wonder she felt exhausted. She followed the two men into the hall.

"Can I give you a lift?" Tom was saying to his friend.

"Don't bother. I'll pick up a taxi along the main road." As though sensing Briony's surprise he added: "My car's being serviced, and won't be ready for a week."

"That's what comes of having expensive foreign makes,"

Tom grinned. "I'd better push off and leave you."

As he disappeared down the corridor, Christopher Clayton leaned against the front door and surveyed Briony in a way that made her uncomfortably aware of herself. "I hope you'll let me see you again?"

"You're very welcome to come here any evening."

"I'd prefer to take you out."

"I don't leave my sister – except to go to the theatre."

"You mean I can only see you if I see Fay?"

He looked so dismayed that Briony smiled. "Sometimes one of the neighbours comes in to look at television with us. I suppose I could get out then."

"That's more like it. What about tomorrow?"

She shook her head and he looked grim. "I've never been made to feel so wanted. How about you and your sister coming to the coast with me on Sunday? If it's nice we can stop off somewhere for lunch."

It was too tempting an offer for Briony to turn down. "It sounds wonderful, Mr. Clayton."

"Christopher," he corrected. "Soon I hope to make it Christopher darling!"

"You don't lack for conceit!"

"I appreciate my sterling worth and I'm going to make sure you do! Till Sunday, bird girl."

She smiled, and was still smiling as she returned to the sitting room, though she was careful to keep her manner casual as she told Fay of Christopher's offer, uncertain what the reaction would be.

But Fay was delighted at the prospect of an outing. "He's so good-looking," she cried. "And I'm sure he's rich. He's got that air of money." She limped towards the bedroom. "He was bowled over by you. I could tell from the minute he saw you."

"Stop romanticising," Briony said firmly. "He's just a

13

friendly young man who's invited us out for the day. There's nothing more to it than that."

"Don't you believe it," Fay said. "Christopher Clayton has fallen for you. Hook, line and sinker."

# CHAPTER TWO

On Sunday Briony awoke with a sense of pleasure at the thought of seeing Christopher Clayton. Fay was excited too, and long before ten o'clock – when he was due to arrive – she was hanging out of the window for a glimpse of him. It was disquieting to think how little it took to make her sister happy, Briony thought. A girl of twenty-three overjoyed at being taken for a drive to the coast!

Sighing, she went into the kitchen to prepare sandwiches, and was just cutting the first slice from a loaf when the doorbell rang. With the knife in her hand she went to open it.

"Well, well," said Christopher Clayton, grinning at her. "I never expected such a bloodthirsty welcome!"

Laughing, she lowered the knife. "You're an hour early."

"I wanted to see what you looked like without goo on your face!"

Her pale skin flushed, and her large grey eyes – as brilliantly glowing without make-up as they were with it – narrowed with embarrassment. "I'm afraid I've gone from the sublime to the ridiculous," she said hurriedly.

He shook his head. "You're beautiful, Briony."

She turned into the kitchen without replying and he followed her, flinging a casual greeting to Fay as he did so.

"Don't tell me you haven't had breakfast?" he said, seeing the bread and various jars on the table.

"I was starting to make the sandwiches," Briony replied.

"Then it's a good thing I got here early. All the food's been provided by courtesy of Fortnum's."

"What sophistication," she said dryly. "I'm sure they've done much better than the egg and tomato sandwiches *I'd* have provided."

"Don't be cross with me." He caught her hand. "I was trying to save you work. This is our first date and I want it to be perfect."

It was impossible to be unmoved by such an apology, and her hurt disappeared. "I'll go and get ready," she said quickly.

Half an hour later they were speeding out of London in a silver grey Citroën which devoured the miles as easily as it did the petrol, and well before noon they were parked on the Sussex Downs, green grass around them, deep blue sky above and deeper blue sea far below.

"It's like a picture postcard," Fay enthused, forgetting her lameness enough to run a few steps to the cliff's edge. "It's stupendous!"

"I wish *you* were as easy to please," Christopher whispered to Briony. "You've been pensive all the way down here. Is anything wrong?"

She hesitated. "I was thinking how little it took to make Fay happy. Not that your taking us out is a little thing. . . ."

"I know what you mean." His voice was unexpectedly gentle as he watched Fay limp back to them and sink down on the grass.

"Food!" she said loudly. "I don't know about you two, but I'm starving."

"Grub's coming up," Christopher said, and taking a hamper from the boot, he spread a gay cloth on the grass and then piled it with food: paté and crusty French rolls, chicken breasts, lobster and assorted salads, chocolate mousse and peaches and two bottles of Moselle.

"Tuck in," he said. "I'm not taking a single crumb back!"

Briony and Fay needed no second bidding. The food was as luscious as it looked and conversation took second place to the pleasure of eating. Only when the cloth was bare except for empty cartons did Christopher take Briony for a stroll along the cliff, leaving Fay dozing on a pile of cushions.

"If the best way to a man's heart is through his stomach,"

16

he said humorously, "the best way to yours is via Fay."

"What does that mean?"

"That if I want to see you again I must keep your sister happy."

"Am I so obvious?"

"You *are* somewhat devoted! If you did less for her she might do more for herself."

"Have you been speaking to Tom?"

"Certainly not." Christopher raised an eyebrow. "I take it *he* thinks so too!"

She nodded and, reluctant to continue the discussion, moved a step ahead of him and peered down. "How smooth the sea looks. Like satin. I can't remember the last time I came to the coast."

"All work and no play makes Jill a dull girl."

"It also makes her a ballet dancer," Briony laughed.

"Is that your only ambition?"

"If it weren't, I'd have given it up long ago. No one remains a dancer unless they love it."

"I must come and watch you. I'm not much of a ballet fan. It's more to Daniel's liking than mine. My brother," he explained at her look.

"Is he an architect too?"

"No. He's a neuro-surgeon. Top man at Luther Hospital."

"He *must* be good."

"He's one of the best in the country." Christopher lit a cigarette. "You wouldn't take us for brothers. He's more like you, in fact – obsessed with his work."

"I'm not obsessed," she protested, "just dedicated."

"It amounts to the same thing. Means you have no time for any life outside your work."

"I found time to come here with you."

"Because you wanted to give Fay an outing."

"I've enjoyed it too," she said.

"Does that mean you'll see me again?"

"If you – if you won't be bored."

"Bored? How little you know your charms!" His hand came out and caught hers, drawing her arm through his as he led her back to Fay.

For most of the return journey Fay dozed in the back of the car and Christopher gave his attention solely to Briony. Yet though he talked a great deal he gave away little about his affairs, and she caught herself wondering why he was still unattached. Perhaps he believed in playing the field. If she saw him again it would be as well to remember this, otherwise she might get hurt.

"You still haven't told me when I can see you again." His voice broke into her thoughts.

"It'll be difficult for the next month. I'm dancing every night."

"Supper then, after the show."

Her face clouded. "It would mean leaving Fay alone too long."

"She can come with us."

"It would make it too late for her. She gets tired easily."

"Then I'll have supper delivered to your flat."

Briony laughed. "Do you always find an answer to everything?"

"Of course." He smoothly changed gear. "We'll make it tomorrow night. Now I've met you, I intend making up for all the wasted years."

Behind them Fay stirred and the conversation became general again until they drew up outside the dilapidated block of flats. Sitting in the gleaming car made Briony painfully aware how shabby the neighbourhood was, and she knew a pang of self-pity. But instantly she pushed it aside and stepped out on to the pavement. Fay clambered out after her, and as her foot touched the ground she gave a gasp and fell.

Instantly Christopher bent and picked her up.

18

"I love women falling at my feet," he grinned. "It does wonders for my ego!"

Fay giggled, her mortification vanishing, and Briony felt a sense of surprise at Christopher's behaviour. His response had been too quick to be calculated, and it made her revise her image of him; he was not pretending to feel sympathy towards Fay in order to worm his way into her own life; he genuinely liked the girl.

As lightly as though Fay were a child he carried her up to the flat and into the bedroom.

"I'm not tired," she protested.

"Yes, you are. It's been a long day for you."

"It's been a long day for me too," Briony said behind them.

"I can take a hint," Christopher smiled, and went through the living room to the front door. "Does Fay often fall down like that?" he asked softly when they were out of earshot.

Briony nodded. "Sometimes she can't even stand."

"Can nothing be done?"

"No one knows the cause. And now she refuses to have any more examinations."

"It must be a heavy burden for you." He put his hands on her shoulders, his beautifully sculptured features softening as he felt their sudden tremble. "Not scared of me, are you? I'd have thought you were used to men holding you."

"It doesn't seem real when you're dancing with them on stage."

"I hope *this* is real for you," he said, and touched his mouth to hers.

Unable to stop herself, she responded to him, and his grip tightened. This was no stage embrace of simulated emotion, for his heart was thudding and the tremor of his body told her of her power over him. Nervously she pushed him away and he slowly dropped his arms to his sides.

"I'll pick you up tomorrow night after the performance,"

he said huskily. "It's going to be wonderful getting to know you."

For the next fortnight Christopher devoted himself to this. Every other evening supper was delivered to their flat by a well-known Soho restaurant, and it was finally left to Fay herself to insist that he and Briony went out by themselves after the theatre, instead of returning to the flat to dine as a threesome.

"I know you have supper here because of me, but if you go on look this I'll feel guilty."

"That's nonsense," Briony protested.

"It's nonsense to pretend you enjoy staying here night after night," Fay retorted.

"I agree," said Christopher. "You're an astute young woman, Fay, and I'll accept your offer." He looked at Briony. "Tomorrow night at the Savoy?"

"It sounds marvellous."

"Briony's never been there," Fay put in. "She's had loads of chances to go out, but she likes sacrificing herself because of me."

"Ungrateful little wench, aren't you?" Christopher teased.

Fay giggled and Briony marvelled at the way her sister responded to him. Relaxed and gay, she looked almost pretty, with her long, pale brown hair and blue eyes seeming twice as large in a face which, though too thin for beauty, nevertheless had its own *gamine* appeal. Her body was not deformed by her lameness and only when she walked did the uneven gait betray itself. But surely this would not condemn her to a life of loneliness? Yet what man could love her when she was in one of her hysterical moods? At times like those even Briony had difficulty in controlling her temper; small wonder that until Christopher's advent, Tom had been the only man able to bother with Fay, though how much this was due to his training as a doctor or to his genuine liking for the girl, Briony did not know.

It was well after midnight when Christopher left, promising to collect Briony at the theatre the following evening and take her straight to the Savoy.

"I've nothing special to wear," she said apologetically, as she saw him to the door.

"With a figure like yours you'd look beautiful in a sack." He kissed her lingeringly on the mouth. "Till tomorrow, my sweet."

But the next day brought a call from him cancelling their evening together.

"My mother's ill," he said seriously, "and I feel I should be with her. She's got a bad heart, and with Daniel in America for the past month she's been gallivanting around more than she should have done. When he's home he watches her like a hawk."

"Don't you?"

"I try. But I don't have the same intimidating effect on her!" His voice deepened. "I'm sorry about tonight, honey, but I'll make up for it tomorrow."

"Don't you think you should wait a few more days and —"

"Mother will be fine by tomorrow. She just needs to rest."

Replacing the telephone, Briony returned to the rehearsal room. But it was hard to make her body buoyant when her mood was so dejected, and she was glad when she was finally able to go to the dressing-room and relax. Only then did she realise how much Christopher meant to her, and the knowledge filled her with fear. He had made no secret of his infatuation for her, yet he had said nothing to make her believe it was anything more than that. Indeed if it was, he would surely have asked her to his home before now; perhaps even suggested she go there tonight? Instantly she dismissed the idea. When he did ask her to meet his mother he would do so when she was well.

Fay endorsed this opinion and added further comment later

that evening. "He's probably waiting till his brother gets back from America too. Then he'll take you home to meet the whole family."

"Why should he have to wait for his brother's return?"

"Because Daniel controls the purse strings. Chris earns a good salary, but the gravy comes from big brother. And he's *very* sparing with it if Chris doesn't toe the line."

"I can't see Christopher taking orders from anyone," Briony said.

"I don't think he would if he were only concerned for himself, but he has to think about his mother too." Seeing her sister's look of puzzlement, Fay added: "Mrs. Clayton is Daniel's *stepmother*. His own mother died when he was three and he was six years old when his father married again. Christopher was born a year later."

"So they're only half-brothers," Briony exclaimed.

"Yes. And big brother was left control of the family fortune. It made him a real dictator. *He* decided which university Chris went to, and once he'd qualified he even told him which firm to join. Chris wanted to set up on his own, but his brother wouldn't –"

"You've made a study of the Clayton family, haven't you?" Briony interrupted dryly.

"Only because Christopher has talked to me a lot while we've been waiting for you each evening. I thought you'd be interested."

"I am. But only in facts – not gossip!"

"It isn't gossip. It's true! Chris wants to marry you – I'm sure of it. But he feels he has to tell his brother first."

Briony could not help but be impressed by what Fay had said, for it explained the fear she had sensed in Christopher whenever his half-brother had been mentioned. If the older man was so autocratic and concerned with prestige, he wasn't going to be pleased when he learned his brother had fallen in love with a ballet dancer. Yet surely when it came to marriage

22

Christopher would not let himself be told what to do – even though his mother's financial well-being was at stake?

Try though she did to reassure herself, Briony lay in bed that night too disturbed to sleep. Unease lay heavy within her, and it remained with her throughout the next day. Christopher was loyal to his family and devoted to his mother; he would not do anything that could affect material comfort, especially since it might also affect her health.

Briony was so convinced she would not be seeing him again that when she came out of the stage door that night and found him waiting for her she flung herself into his arms with an abandon she had not shown before.

"Looks as if I should stay away from you more often," he joked as he led her to his car. "You've no idea how much I missed you. Mother kept asking me last night why I was so edgy."

"What did you tell her?"

An oncoming car held his attention, and when next he spoke it was on a different subject. "Do you know this is the first time we've been alone for ages?"

"I'm surprised you still bother with me."

"You're worth waiting for."

"Am I?"

He caught her hand to his lips. "Any other girl with your looks and figure would know the answer to that. You're adorable, Briony." His foot slackened on the accelerator and then he increased speed. "No, if I stop now and start kissing you we'll never get to the Savoy!"

Briony gave a laugh of pure happiness and was still bubbling with it when they entered the brightly lit restaurant. In a simple black crêpe dress, the only long one she possessed and which she had bought because she had known its simplicity would prevent it from dating, she looked her most ethereal. Devoid of make-up except for a faint touch of lipstick and mascara, her skin had the creamy glow of a pearl, making the delicate tracery of blue veins at her throat and wrists more noticeable. Her hair was no longer confined in a restricted chignon but combed loosely away from her high forehead to fall in a thick amber cloud to her shoulders.

"It's the colour of a toffee apple," Christopher said, leading her on to the dance floor. "I never realised it until now. You should always wear it like that."

"Madame Cassini would have a fit. She'd like me to dye it black and pretend to be Russian!"

"Don't you dare!" He pulled her closer. "You seem taller than usual. Have you grown?"

"My shoes have!" She lifted her skirt to disclose high wedges.

"That's cheating," he protested. "I like to think of you as my little treasure."

She thrilled at his tone, her look of delight showing him plainly how she felt.

It was well after midnight when they left the Savoy, but instead of heading for home Christopher parked the car beside the Embankment. Street lamps threw pools of light on the dark pavement, though the light did not touch the river which, only reflecting the sickle moon, gleamed like a dark ribbon in front of them. For several moments Christopher said nothing and Briony — aware of an unusual tenseness about him — remained motionless. Then with a stifled exclamation he pulled her close, one hand twining round her hair, and the other caressing her body, awakening her to a fierce response that thrilled and frightened her.

"I was so proud of you tonight," he whispered. "You were the most beautiful woman in the restaurant."

"*You* were the most handsome man," she whispered back, and half turned her head away from his seeking lips.

But he was not to be dissuaded, and he stroked her body again, his hand moving down her slender back. "I love you, Briony. You're everything I've dreamed of. You've got to come away with me. I want you. . . ."

"And I want *you*," she whispered. "But I –"

"No buts," he said fiercely, and tugged at the fragile shoulder straps on her shoulders. The flimsy fabric gave way and fell, disclosing the pearly outline of her breasts. "You're beautiful," he muttered. "I won't have any peace till you're mine."

These were the words she had longed to hear, and she was filled with happiness. It gave her the strength to push him away and to keep him away as he tried to catch her close.

"Don't fight," he pleaded. "I want you. Come away with me."

"I can't. It – it wouldn't be right."

"But we love each other!"

"That's the reason I can't." Seeing his surprise, she said: "I love you too much to spoil it. When I'm yours I want it to be without any reservation, without the slightest feeling that I'm doing wrong."

"What's wrong about making love?" She did not answer and he peered at her. "Darling, I do believe you're old-fashioned!"

"I'm afraid I am. Are you sorry?"

"Of course not." He pressed his lips to her palm. "I'm glad in a way. Though it won't stop me from trying to make you change your mind."

It was nearly dawn before Briony let herself into the flat. The hours of lovemaking, with desire never wholly appeased, had left her enervated, and the moment her head touched the pillow she fell fast asleep.

Luckily the next day was Sunday and she was able to wake up at leisure and potter round the flat. Fay was eager to hear all that happened and Briony described the food and the decor at the Savoy, but omitted the hours she had spent with Christopher in the car.

"I'd love to go to the Savoy," Fay breathed. "It sounds like heaven."

"I'll get Christopher to take us there one night if you feel up to it."

"Why shouldn't I feel up to it?" Instantly Fay was on the defensive. "Stop treating me like an invalid all the time! Christopher says I need to get out more, that I shouldn't be cooped up in the flat all day."

"You know you find it hard to go down the stairs," Briony said quietly.

"One day we'll live in a house *without* stairs. A bungalow in the country on the Sussex Downs where I can have a separate wing and not be a burden on you."

Briony looked at her sister sharply. She was used to Fay's day-dreams, but this talk of a bungalow in the country sounded as if it stemmed from a more concrete basis – as if it had been discussed as an actual possibility. Yet with whom could Fay have discussed such a thing? Instantly Christopher came to mind, and though reluctant to test her belief, the more she thought about it the more convinced she became that he must have encouraged Fay to think in terms of a better and happier future. A future for the three of them!

Almost bursting with joy, Briony whisked through her cleaning of the flat, and was doing the final dusting, when the object of her happy thoughts appeared to take them for their usual Sunday drive in the country.

This time when he brought them home Fay went to her room without being told, as though aware Christopher and Briony longed to be alone, and hardly had the door closed on her when they were in each other's arms, mouth against mouth, thigh against thigh.

"When can we be alone together?" he whispered.

"I don't know."

"I've got to get you to myself," he said hoarsely. "I can't sleep for thinking of you."

26

"I'm the same," she said, edging him to the door.

"Then why are you trying to get rid of me?" he teased. "It's barely midnight."

"I've an early call for rehearsal. While you're dozing in front of your drawing-board I'll be at the barre."

"Every time I doze I dream of you and wake up more dissatisfied and tired than ever!"

"You'd better drink hot milk," she smiled. "It's excellent for night starvation."

"Beast!" he said, but before he could catch hold of her again she pushed him out and closed the door, calling a final goodnight through the letter box.

# CHAPTER THREE

ARRIVING at the theatre on Monday morning Briony was told she was going to dance the role of the Lilac Fairy.

"But I'm not ready for it," she stammered to Madame Cassini.

"Oleg Beloff says you are."

Since Oleg Beloff was the artistic director of the company, Briony was silenced, though her fears remained.

"Don't just stand there," Madame Cassini went on. "Go to the wardrobe mistress for a fitting and then meet me in the rehearsal room. And be prepared to stay late for the rest of the week. You will need all the rehearsal you can get if you don't want to turn Friday night into a fiasco!"

Knowing the ballet mistress too well to take notice of her pessimistic portents, Briony scuttled off to see about her costume, and it was not until lunchtime that she was able to telephone Fay with her news and say she was too busy to go to Mr. Van de Heim to collect some more jewellery.

"I'll go myself," Fay said. "I feel fine today. And stop worrying about me. Think of *your* wonderful future instead!"

Briony was still trying to do this when, weary in mind as well as muscle, she let herself into the flat that evening. It was a good thing she had refused to see Christopher until the end of the week. Even the thought of talking to Fay was exhausting.

"You'll never guess what Chris has done," Fay greeted her excitedly. "He's booked tickets for Friday night's performance and he's taking *me*. Then we'll all go to the Savoy afterwards to celebrate!"

Pleasure at Christopher's action brought tears to Briony's eyes, but she blinked them away as Fay dangled a ruby and gold necklace in front of her.

28

"Mr. Van de Heim's given me this to repair. Isn't it gorgeous?"

"It looks very valuable."

"It's worth three thousand pounds."

"And he let you bring it back here?"

"It's insured, silly. A couple of the stones need re-setting." Fay put the necklace back in its velvet box. "I bought some mushrooms to make an omelette. I'll go and do it."

"Let me." With an effort Briony forced back her tiredness and stood up, but Fay pushed her back into the chair and limped out.

Surprisingly soon Fay called her into the kitchen where she found the table laid and two delicious omelettes set out. It had been a long time since she had found Fay in such good spirits, and she realised how much of her sister's lassitude came from being cooped up in the flat. Yet only rarely did she volunteer to go out by herself as she had done today, and Briony knew that the confidence stemmed from Christopher. As though she had conjured him up, he telephoned her.

"I miss not seeing you," he grumbled. "But I'm being good and staying with Mother."

"Is she better?"

"A little. But she misses Daniel."

"He isn't her son."

Christopher laughed. "I sometimes think she likes him more than me." His voice deepened. "I don't mind as long as I've got all *your* love."

"You know you have."

"I'm going to come round and see you," he said at once.

"I'm too tired."

"Just for half an hour," he pleaded.

"No, darling. Wait till Friday."

"Very well," he whispered, "but only because you're exhausted. Goodnight, my darling. I'm counting the hours till I can see you again."

By the end of the week Briony was in a state of panic at her impending ordeal. She left early for the theatre, glad that Christopher had offered to collect Fay, and spent the entire afternoon rehearsing again.

Waiting in the wings as the auditorium slowly filled, she doubted that her shaking legs would carry her on to the stage, but when the inevitable happened and she danced into the spotlight, all trace of nerves disappeared and she was conscious of nothing other than this moment in time. There was no past, no future, just the wonderful dancing present when she glided and pirouetted on waves of music.

She took her bow to loud applause, and returning to the wings burst into tears that increased as several young dancers clustered round to congratulate her.

She was still tearful from nervous reaction as she entered the Savoy restaurant later with Christopher and Fay. This time they had a table near the entrance which, though less secluded, meant Fay did not have to walk so far.

"Christopher's ordered the meal too," Fay burbled as she sat down and undid her jacket.

Briony gave him a warm smile and for the first time noticed how pale he was. Evidently he had been suffering from nerves too! She stretched out her hand to him, but he did not appear to see the gesture and her hand dropped to her side.

"You were fantastic, Briony," Fay went on. "I didn't go out during the interval, but Chris said everybody was talking about you."

"They were." Christopher looked directly into Briony's eyes. "You were great. The best I've ever seen."

"You once said you were no judge of ballet," she reminded him with a smile.

"Your brother is, though, isn't he?" Fay intervened. "I read in this morning's paper that he's returned from America."

"He flew back last night," Christopher said. "A week earlier than we'd expected. He'd planned to spend a holiday

30

with friends, but when he heard Mother was ill, he came home."

"He must be as kind as you!" Briony said.

"That's not an adjective I'd normally apply to him. If he doesn't get his own way he can be. . . ." Christopher braced his shoulders. "Let's not talk about my family tonight. I'd rather talk about you. What will your future be now, Briony?"

She grinned. "Longer practice hours and a five-pound rise!"

"I refuse to believe such pessimism," Fay declared, and flung her jacket off. Only then did the ruby and gold necklace come into view round her throat, and seeing Briony's eyes on it, she flushed. "I – I only borrowed it for tonight."

"I wish you hadn't. It's so valuable."

"It's safer on me than leaving it at home!"

"It's my fault really," said Christopher. "Fay was putting it away when I arrived, and it looked so beautiful I insisted she wore it."

"It transforms this awful old dress," Fay put in.

Briony's anger faded. If borrowed plumes made Fay feel better able to face the world, what right did she have to reproach her?

"It does look lovely," she admitted. "One day I'll buy you one of your own."

Fay gripped her hand in delight. "That's the first time *you've* indulged in day-dreaming! Just listen to her, Christopher."

"I am," he said with a slight smile.

"Why don't you both dance?" Fay asked.

"I'm sure Briony's danced enough for one night."

His words increased Briony's feeling that something was wrong. The last time they had come here he had harboured no such thoughts. Yet now, when her dancing had been less arduous – albeit more nerve-racking – he was refusing the chance of taking her in his arms. Certain that his behaviour

31

was connected with his brother's homecoming, she was relieved when they finally returned to the flat, and Fay, unaware of the tension in the atmosphere and still hugging her jacket around her, limped happily off to bed.

Only as the door closed and Briony was alone with Christopher did she ask him what was wrong. "Don't pretend nothing's the matter," she said firmly, "because I know there is."

"I wasn't going to pretend," he replied nervously. "You'd have had to know sooner or later. But I don't know how to begin."

"Does it concern your brother?"

"It *shouldn't* concern him," Christopher said bitterly, "except that he's made my whole life his concern."

Briony swallowed. "I suppose he doesn't like you going out with a dancer!"

"It's got nothing to do with your dancing. Nothing!" Christopher stepped into the centre of the room. The light shone down on his head, turning his hair to gold, and she closed her eyes against the sight.

"Are you frightened of your brother?" she whispered.

There was a long pause.

"Not for myself," he said at last. "But I have to consider my mother. When my father died he left Daniel in control of everything. He's never abused that control, but he would if he had to. Tonight he made it clear that I have to obey his orders."

"What can he do if you refuse? You've a successful career of your own. He couldn't spoil that."

"My salary isn't enough to keep my mother in the same way that Daniel does. And he's made it very clear that if I don't do as he wants, he'll make things difficult for her. Don't get Daniel wrong," he went on quickly. "He's been exceptionally generous to my mother, but –"

"He'll take away her security if you don't obey him?"

"Yes."

She swallowed convulsively. "I don't understand. If he doesn't object to my being a ballet dancer, why else does he want you to stop seeing me?"

Christopher lit a cigarette. He drew in a lungful of smoke, expelled it and then stubbed the cigarette out. "There's something you should know. Until you do, the rest won't make any sense. When I saw Tom that first night it was only because I – I was at a loose end. That morning my – my fiancée had gone for a holiday to Australia with her parents."

Briony caught the back of a chair to steady herself. "*Your fiancée?*"

"Yes," he muttered. "I should have told you at the beginning, but I – I thought that –"

"I was a pick-up you could drop when it suited you?" she burst out.

"Don't!" he cried. "From the moment I met you I wasn't *capable* of thinking! You were the loveliest girl I'd seen and –"

"Stop it!" she cried. "You talk about me as if I were a statue. But I'm a woman – not something to be dropped like a doll when you're tired of playing with it."

"Briony," there was an agony of remorse in his voice, "I love you."

"If that was true you'd break your engagement."

"And have Daniel turn my mother out of the house?"

"I don't believe he would. He couldn't deliberately destroy the happiness of a woman who's been like a mother to him."

"He'll do anything to stop me breaking my engagement to Maureen."

"Why?" Briony demanded.

"Because her father's Sir Geoffrey Hirst – Chairman of the Board of Governors of the Luther Hospital."

Briony frowned. "Why is that important for him?"

"Because Daniel has set his heart on getting a neurological
33

wing built, and Sir Geoffrey's the one man who can push it through."

"You mean he'll sacrifice your happiness for.... No, I don't believe it!"

"It's true. His work is his life and he's set his heart on having the most up-to-date neurological centre in the world. He's convinced that if it's built the way he wants it – with a special theatre and after-care units – that he'll be able to perform operations no one's yet succeeded in doing."

"You're making out a good case for him," she said coldly. "But no matter how you dress it up it still amounts to personal ambition."

"It's much more than ambition," Christopher persisted. "He really believes he has a gift as a surgeon and he's determined to use it to the best of his ability."

"To the best of *your* ability, you mean!" Briony said bitterly.

"What can I do?" Christopher begged. "If he uses my mother as a threat.... For heaven's sake, Briony, you've got to see my position?"

"I do, only too well." She moved away from the chair as though she no longer needed its support. "You'd better go. There's no more to be said."

"I can't leave like this," he cried. "There must be something I can do."

"You've already done enough. Making a fool of me was pretty despicable, but fooling Fay.... Did you *have* to let her believe we were going to live in a bungalow in the country? It was cruel to pretend with *her*. Cruel and heartless!"

"I was hoping things would change ... that something would happen. Oh, God!" He kicked at the carpet, the gesture making him look like a little boy being punished for something he did not understand.

With an effort Briony retained her composure. "Please go. There's nothing more to be said."

"But I've got to see you again."

"No, never!"

Christopher half moved towards her, then he drew back. "Goodbye, darling," he whispered. "Please forgive me."

His steps receded across the room to the hall. The front door closed and there was silence. Only then did Briony give way to her misery, and sinking on to the settee, she burst into tears. So much for the bright future she had dreamed of. The bungalow in the country with a special wing for Fay had been destroyed to make way for a special wing for Daniel Clayton; a wing to satisfy his vanity as a surgeon.

"I hate him!" she cried aloud. "I hate him!"

It took Fay longer than Briony to accept what had occurred. Coming in to see why her sister had not yet come to bed, she had found her dissolved in tears, and it had taken only a moment to learn the entire story.

"But Chris loves you," she had cried. "I can't believe it!"

"He loves his mother too. And he can't let his brother ruin her life."

"What about the way he's ruining yours? Surely Chris must have known what his brother would do? Why didn't he tell you he was engaged?" Fay's voice had risen with anger. "He's as bad as Daniel Clayton. Worse, in fact!"

"There isn't much to choose between either of them," Briony had agreed, "and if you don't mind, I'd rather not talk about them any more. I want to pretend they don't exist."

"You won't forget Christopher so easily."

"Who said it would be easy?"

"Briony, I –"

"No more conversation. It's over and I don't want to discuss it."

For all Briony's determination to put Christopher out of her mind, the only time she was able to do so was when she was dancing. Luckily her success as the Lilac Fairy brought her further roles to study, and this necessitated even longer hours at the barre under Madame Cassini's piercing glance.

If she had only had herself to think of, Briony would have spent every hour at the theatre driving her body to the limit of endurance so that her head would hold no thought apart from the aching of her limbs. But there was always Fay to consider, and her sister's drawn face and red-rimmed eyes worried her so much that she always returned to the flat the moment she could each evening.

"I know you're finding it more and more difficult to walk these days," she finally expostulated one night when she came home and found Fay still huddled in her dressing-gown. "But you'll make yourself ill if you don't get *any* fresh air."

"I don't want to go out."

"You must make the effort. Forget what Christopher did. He isn't worth thinking about."

"I'm *not* thinking about him." Fay huddled forward and began to cry. "It's worse. Much worse."

"What's worse? Tell me," Briony pleaded. "Is it Mr. Van der Heim? Doesn't he want you to work for him any more?"

At this Fay cried even harder, rocking backwards and forwards in an agony of despair. "I wish I were dead! It's the only way out."

"Nothing can be as bad as that!" Briony was horrified by the outburst. "For heaven's sake tell me what it is."

"It's the necklace," Fay sobbed. "The ruby and gold one. I've lost it."

"Lost it?" Briony caught her breath. "How? When?"

"The night we went to the Savoy. When we got back home I found it had gone."

"Why didn't you tell me at once?"

"Because of Christopher," Fay gulped. "You were already upset because of him and I didn't want to make things worse."

With an effort Briony held on to her temper. "What did you do?"

"First thing next morning I went to the Savoy. The manager had a thorough search made, but they couldn't find it. I even went to the theatre, but –"

"You had it on in the restaurant," Briony interrupted. "You must have dropped it on the way out to the car." She gripped Fay's arm. "Have you called the police?"

"No. I was frightened to. If I do that they'll go to Mr. Van der Heim and tell him."

"You mean he doesn't know?"

"Of course he doesn't! Once he finds out he'll put me in prison!" Fay burst into another storm of tears. "I keep telling him I haven't mended it, but I can't stall for ever." Her voice rose, thready with hysteria. "It's Christopher's fault. He talked me into wearing it. I'd never have done if it hadn't been for him!"

"You can't blame Christopher. You're not a child, Fay. You knew exactly what you were doing."

"But he encouraged me. Oh, Briony, what can I do?"

"Tell Mr. Van der Heim and then the police. After that it will be up to the insurance company. Your losing the necklace was an accident and they'll have to pay up. I doubt if you'll ever be able to work for a jeweller again, but –"

"The necklace wasn't insured," Fay interrupted, her voice anguished.

For an instant Briony was not sure she had heard correctly, but one look at the white face in front of her and she knew she had.

"But Mr. Van der Heim told you it was insured! I remember asking you about it."

"It's insured when it's in his shop and when it's with me – here in the flat – but it isn't covered for anywhere else. The only person who's insured to wear it is the owner."

The news was so shattering that Briony found it difficult to speak. "If that's . . . then it means . . . then *we're* responsible. Legally as well as morally."

"Yes." Fay's voice was shrill. "Now you see why it's so awful. If the owner prosecutes me for negligence I can be sent to prison!"

"No one's going to prosecute you," Briony said with a conviction she did not feel. "I'll tell Mr. Van der Heim *I* was wearing it."

"What good will that do? They'll put *you* in prison instead!"

"Stop talking about prison," Briony insisted. "You're not a thief."

"You are if you borrow something without permission. What am I going to do?"

"Leave it to me. I'll talk to Oleg Beloff first thing in the morning. If he'll advance me six months' salary I can give Mr. Van der Heim five hundred pounds straight away."

"If only you can," Fay gasped. "He'll still be furious, but at least he'd know his client will eventually get the money. Oh, Briony, I'm so glad you know the truth. I'm sure we can work things out."

Briony was far less sanguine. To pay for the necklace would take her years of arduous work, and the knowledge hung over her like a shroud, overlaying her every action and thought.

Though she had been dreading her meeting with Mr. Van der Heim, it was the one with Oleg Beloff which turned out to be the worst.

"I am already juggling like a madman to pay the wages bill each *week*," he said curtly. "To pay you six months in advance is out of the question. A month perhaps, but not more than that." His narrow Polish face tightened with sympathy. "You have had many problems with your sister. It is time she learned to stand on her own feet."

"If she had two good feet I'd let her."

"I know about her lameness," he sighed. "You feel things too deeply, child, that is your trouble. Still, that's one reason why you are such a good dancer."

"I'm not sure I'll be able to continue," she said slowly. "I've got to pay off three thousand pounds and I can't have the prospect hanging over me for years."

"No other company will pay you more than I do," Beloff said.

"I wasn't thinking of going to another company." Briony turned and caught sight of her reflection in the mirror behind the ballet director's head. She had always taken her appearance for granted and even Christopher's compliments about her beauty had not impinged on her until this moment when she was faced with a decision that only she could resolve. Coolly she tried to assess her looks. No voluptuous beauty in the exaggerated standards of Hollywood, she nevertheless had the insidious appeal that came from delicacy of line and a deceptive air of fragility. With her thick amber-gold hair loosened and a more skilful use of make-up, there were not many men who would pass her by unnoticed.

"What else can you do?" Oleg Beloff asked irritably. "You have trained all your life as a dancer, how much more would you earn as a typist?"

She smiled faintly. "I wasn't thinking of working in an office. There are plenty of clubs that need hostesses."

"You?" Beloff said sarcastically. "Your future is here. Your career is just beginning. You will go far."

"It's kind of you to say so," she said politely.

"I am not being kind. I am stating a fact." His eyes narrowed so that the lines around them increased, making him look near his real age of fifty than the forty he pretended. "You will be a prima ballerina, Briony. But you must be patient. Months ago I picked you out as my next star. Madame Cassini knows it – that's why she pushes you to the limits all the time. You are a good dancer now, but one day soon you will be a great one!"

Briony swallowed hard, afraid she would dissolve into tears. "It's too late for me. I can't stay on here."

39

"You *must*. I'm not letting you throw yourself away for a paltry three thousand."

"It isn't paltry when you don't have it."

"Let me talk to this jeweller."

The offer was so unexpected that she blinked. Never had she known Beloff involve himself in the affairs of anyone, let alone an insignificant member of the company. Yet she wasn't insignificant, she reminded herself. If what he said was true, she was going to be extremely important to him.

"If only I could raise the money myself," he muttered. "But with my present overdraft it is out of the question. I'll go and see this jeweller now," he reiterated. "You go to the practice room and start work." He pulled Briony to her feet and pushed her out of the door. "Practise," he repeated, "and leave everything else to me!"

Out in the corridor Briony leaned weakly against the wall. This was the first time that anyone apart from Tom had tried to shoulder some of her responsibility. The shroud began to lift and she glimpsed a lightening of the future. Happier than at any time since she had learned the truth about Christopher, she ran down to the practice room.

# CHAPTER FOUR

FOR the rest of the day Briony forced herself not to think about the necklace, but as she stood in the wings at seven o'clock it returned to her mind with full force. What would happen if Oleg Beloff couldn't persuade Mr. Van der Heim to accept delayed payments for the necklace? Beneath her vivid theatrical make-up her skin paled. The Dutchman *had* to see reason. It would be too cruel if she had to give up ballet when she had her foot on the first step to fame.

Even if she had married Christopher she would not have given up dancing. It was not only a way of life, it was part of her very existence. She drew a deep breath and pulled her cardigan more closely around her shoulders.

It was odd that during their many conversations she and Christopher had never talked about this aspect of her life. But then he had always kept the future nebulous, making it sound hopeful and joyous yet somehow intangible, like a spider's web that glistened like diamonds in front of you yet turned to nothing when you caught hold of it.

"Briony!"

She turned to see Oleg Beloff beside her, his overcoat still slung over his shoulders.

"You've seen Mr. Van der Heim?" she asked breathlessly.

"I might have saved myself the trouble. The necklace has already been paid for."

"Paid for?" she was incredulous. "I don't understand. Who would do *that*?"

"Your sister. She went there this afternoon with two thousand five hundred pounds."

"*Fay* paid him?"

"Yes. She rang and told me she'd done so, but I didn't

41

believe her, so I went to see Van der Heim for myself."

"But why did she ring *you*?"

"After you left my office this morning I tried to look up the man's address. But there are so many ways of spelling his name that I finally called your sister. She seemed surprised I'd offered to help you and I made it clear I wasn't going to let you destroy everything you've worked for by becoming a Bunny Girl!"

"You shouldn't have told her that."

"Well, I did." His grin was wolfish. "She almost had hysterics on the phone and said she'd call me back with Van der Heim's address."

"But she knows it by heart!"

Beloff shrugged. "It was an hour before she called. And then it was to tell me she'd got most of the money and was going there herself."

"But where did she get it from? We haven't even got anything to pawn! I must call her and find out."

"You're not calling anybody until after the show."

Only years of training saw Briony through that evening's performance. With her mind elsewhere she relied solely on technique, and drew a sour look from Madame Cassini as she came off stage. Hurrying to the dressing-room, she slipped into a black leotard and without pausing to take off her make-up, rushed from the theatre.

As though she had been alert for Briony's footsteps Fay was waiting by the front door. She was dressed for bed, but her face was far from sleepy, and her eyes sparkled with triumph and defiance.

Too overwrought to bother with diplomacy, Briony caught her by the hand and pulled her into the living room.

"Where did you get the money to pay Mr. Van der Heim? I want the truth, Fay. None of your lies!"

"Christopher gave it to me."

The answer was so unexpected – yet so obvious – that

Briony was astonished she had not thought of it herself. She sank on to a chair and stared at Fay as though looking at a stranger. "Why did he give it to you? He must know we won't be able to pay him back for years."

"There's no question of paying it back. He's given us the money."

"You're lying!"

"Ring him up and ask him." Then hastily: "No, you'd better not. I promised him we wouldn't contact him again. That was part – part of the arrangement."

The hesitation in Fay's voice did not go unnoticed. "Part of what arrangement? Christopher didn't give you the money just because you asked him. There's more to it than that."

"I don't know why you think so. A couple of thousand doesn't mean anything to him."

"It means a great deal," Briony corrected. "It's his brother who has money, not Christopher."

"Well, he didn't have any trouble finding some. Anyway, he was pleased to pay for the necklace. He said he felt responsible for my losing it."

"You can't blame Christopher for that," Briony said angrily, and stood up.

The knowledge that they were in debt to him was far worse than being indebted to the jeweller or Oleg Beloff. At least with them the transaction would have been an entirely business one. But borrowing the money from Christopher – regardless of what Fay said she had no intention of accepting it as a gift – meant he would be in her mind until the loan was repaid. And that could take years!

"I don't know why you're angry with me." Fay was sullen now, playing the injured party and enjoying it. "I thought you'd be pleased at what I'd done. When Mr. Beloff said you were threatening to give up ballet I couldn't stand by and do nothing."

"Mr. Beloff was going to talk to Mr. Van der Heim."

"Do you think that would have stopped him for prosecuting me? *You* might be scared of Beloff because he owns the ballet company, but he means nothing in Mr. Van der Heim's life! All that mattered to him was having the necklace back or the money."

"I know you acted for the best," Briony said, "but I can't be indebted to Christopher."

"Why not? He deserves to pay for all the misery he caused you. I should have asked him for double!"

"Fay!" Briony was horrified at the venom in her sister's voice. But before she could say any more the doorbell rang. The sound was so unexpected that she jumped with fright. Who on earth could be calling at midnight?

"It must be Tom," she said, and running across the hall, flung open the door.

A man stood looking at her. A man with a pale skin and thick, reddish brown hair. Though only average height he was so broad-shouldered that he seemed to tower over her. Or perhaps she had this impression because of the menacing look of his thin mouth and the fury in his eyes. Hazel eyes that reminded her of Christopher.

"I'm Daniel Clayton," he said coldly. "May I come in?"

Briony stepped back and he entered the hall and closed the door. His eyes never left her face and only as she saw his mouth turn down even more sharply did she realise the sight she must look in her skin-tight leotard and garish make-up. Surely he didn't think she usually wore peacock blue eye-shadow and inch-long eyelashes?

"I want to talk to you." His voice was surprisingly quiet for such a large, well-built man, but though quiet it had the hardness of steel.

Unwilling to take him into the sitting-room and subject Fay to a further scene, Briony remained where she was. "If you have anything to say to me, you can say it here. I don't want to upset my sister."

"I'm glad there's one member of your family that can be upset by what I might say!"

"Spare me your sarcasm, Mr. Clayton, and tell me why you're here."

"As if you don't know!" he said harshly. "I heard your phone call to my brother."

"*My* call?"

"Yes. I had picked up the telephone in another part of the house and before I could put it down I heard you talking to him – or perhaps blackmailing is a better word."

Briony stared at him in amazement. Surely he hadn't misconstrued Fay's plea for help as blackmail?

"Blackmail," Daniel Clayton repeated. "When I heard what you were saying I listened in to the rest of the conversation. When it finished I went to tell Christopher not to give you a penny, but by the time I got downstairs he'd already left the house. When he came back I made him tell me the whole story." He came a step closer. "Christopher may believe this is your last demand for money, but *I* don't. That's why I'm here. To tell you that from now on *I'm* concerning myself with his future, and if you want to tell Maureen the truth, go ahead and do so!"

Listening to the tirade Briony felt like a non-swimmer who had plunged into the deep end of a pool and was floundering around in a sea of words. Only as he continued to speak did the sentences make sense. Horrifying, appalling sense. Fay had lied about her conversation with Christopher. She had not pleaded for money, but threatened for it; demanded it in exchange for not telling Christopher's fiancée what had happened in her absence.

"Did Christopher say it was *me* on the phone?" she asked slowly.

"I didn't need to ask him the obvious." Daniel Clayton looked at her with dislike. "Your words gave you away."

Still unwilling to implicate Fay, she stared at the floor.

45

"What did Christopher tell you about me?"

"He confirmed what I had already learned from my mother."

"She knows?" Briony could not hide her surprise.

"Some friends of ours saw you both at the Savoy. When my mother asked him who you were, he said a friend. And also that you knew he was engaged." Daniel Clayton's pale face grew paler, making his hair look redder than it was. "When I reminded Christopher of this he admitted he'd made a fool of himself over you — said he hadn't believed you'd make him pay for his fun."

Briony swayed and the light bulb above her head grew bright and dim and bright again. "He . . . he said that?" she whispered, and could say no more, appalled by what she had heard. Yet what hope did she have of making this cynical, furious man believe that it was Christopher who had behaved badly? Her eyes filled with tears as she thought of him. She could forgive him for lying to his mother about her, but she could never forgive him for not telling his brother the truth. How dared he pretend he had been the victim of a scheming gold-digger? And then to let Daniel Clayton think it had been her on the phone and not Fay.

Even as she thought of this she knew the answer. Only by turning her into the scapegoat could Christopher come out of the situation with his own character intact. He was obviously afraid of incurring his brother's anger. The purse strings evidently bound Christopher too.

With an effort Briony forced herself to speak again. "Knowing the sort of girl I am, aren't you afraid I might take you at your word and go and see Christopher's fiancée?"

"It wouldn't matter if you did. One look at your face and she'd know the sort of girl you are!"

Briony's hand swung out, but before it could make contact with the face in front of her it was caught in an iron grip. "Oh no, you don't," the man grated. "You've met your match in

46

me!" He flung her hand away so violently that she staggered. "I'll say what I came here to say, and then I'll go. Keep away from my family, Miss Stevens. That means Christopher and my stepmother. If you try and hurt them I won't be responsible for my actions! Do I make myself clear?"

"More than clear," she cried. "But you can't fool me. You're not here because you care about your family. All you're concerned with is making sure that your brother marries Sir Geoffrey Hirst's daughter! It would put paid to all *your* plans if he didn't!"

"My plans are *my* concern." His voice held a quiet menace that made her shiver. "All I am telling you is to keep away from my stepmother and Christopher."

"And if I don't?"

His hand went into his pocket and she recoiled with fear. But when he drew it out it held a cheque book. "How much more do you need to mend your broken heart?"

Sickened, she stared at the cheque book.

"How much?" he repeated. "Another two thousand five hundred? Five thousand for a fortnight's pretence of love is a high rate even for the oldest profession in the world!"

This was the final insult, and Briony's anguish hardened into fury. If he believed her to be that sort of person then she would act as one. Let him sweat with fear for the next few minutes. Let him discover what it was like to be at the receiving end of a merciless tongue!

"Do you think I'd be satisfied with five thousand?" she mocked. "I wouldn't even accept double!"

"I've no intention of increasing my offer."

"I don't want money," she replied. "I want marriage!"

"Christopher will never marry you. He loves Maureen."

"You believe him?" she taunted.

"Yes." There was a pause as though he was wondering whether to continue. Then he pulled at his lip and spoke. "When Christopher got home tonight and I tackled him about
47

you, he broke down and cried. Yes – cried! Not for love of you, Miss Stevens, but because he's afraid Maureen will find out and not want him any more!"

No words could have hurt Briony more than these. Not only did they destroy any hope she might have had of Christopher returning to her, but they tolled the death knell for the man himself: for the man she had believed him to be.

"Perhaps now you will accept my offer," Daniel Clayton went on. "Shall we say a total of five thousand?"

"How dare you talk to Briony like that?" a shrill voice cried, and Fay darted into the hall. "Your brother's a liar and a cheat, and no money on earth can make up for what he did!"

"Fay!" Briony stepped over to her sister, but was pushed away with surprising strength.

"Why shouldn't he know the truth? Why do you just stand there and let him accuse you like that?" She swung round to Daniel Clayton. "Christopher wasn't just having a good time with Briony, he wanted to marry her. And he *would* have done if he hadn't been scared of you! And then you come here offering us money." Fay's voice rose. "How far do you think five thousand pounds will go today?"

"It wasn't my intention to set you both up for life," came the icy reply. "You appear to have the same grandiose ideas as your sister."

"What do you know about our ideas? All you know is what Christopher told you – and everything he said was a lie! A lie!" she screamed, and then screamed again and again, peal after peal that rang through the flat like the cry of a wild thing.

The man drew back, his expression startled. Then as the shrill monotony of the screams continued, an odd look passed over his face and he took a step forward. But Briony was there before him, clutching at Fay's arm and glancing at him over her shoulder.

"I must call Tom – our doctor."

"I'm a doctor," he said, and leaning forward slapped Fay hard across the face.

A peal stopped in mid-sound, wavered and died like a bird shot on the wing. Grey eyes which a moment ago had been blank took on life again and glittered with tears that spilled and overflowed down the waxy cheeks.

All anger gone, Briony cradled Fay against her, but Daniel Clayton pushed her aside and, swinging the girl up into his arms as though she weighed nothing, carried her into the living-room and set her on the settee.

"A glass of hot water," he murmured to Briony.

She ran to obey him, returning with a filled cup into which he dissolved the contents of a capsule.

Fay looked as though she were going to refuse it, but the man's expression brooked no argument, and making a face at the bitter taste she gulped the liquid down. "What was it?"

"A sedative. Do you often have hysterics?"

Fay did not answer and he stepped back from the settee and looked at Briony. "Get your sister to bed. We'll finish our conversation another time.

"Christopher ruined our lives and he should pay for it," Fay interrupted.

"I was under the impression he went out with your sister." Daniel Clayton was no longer the surgeon but an angry man defending his brother.

"He spent a lot of time with me when he was waiting for Briony. That's when he told me about the bungalow in the country and the separate flat he'd build on it for *me*." Again the thin voice rose, but this time hysteria did not take hold, for the barbiturate was working and the glitter in the eyes began to lessen as the eyes themselves found it difficult to focus. "I'm tired," Fay said plaintively, and standing up, limped into the bedroom.

Briony looked at Daniel Clayton. "Please go."

He hesitated, his eyes – so like Christopher's – glittering like tourmaline. Then in silence he turned on his heel and went out. As the front door closed, Fay called from the bedroom and Briony went in to see her at once.

"You should try and go to sleep," she murmured. "It's late."

"I have to talk to you first. I'm sorry about what happened tonight. I know I shouldn't have threatened Christopher, but he was so horrid when he heard my voice that I lost my temper."

"He was probably scared when you rang him."

"Why should he have been? I was only going to ask him to lend us a couple of hundred pounds. Just enough for us to show Mr. Van der Heim we intended paying for the necklace. But he never even gave me a chance to explain. He started to shout and call me names, and I got so angry that I said the first thing that came into my head. That's why I asked him for *all* the money. If he could think I was wicked enough to make trouble for him, then he deserved trouble!"

"Two wrongs don't make a right."

"Rubbish!" Fay stretched and yawned. "I got the money, didn't I?"

"The price we paid for it was rather high." Briony tried to keep the bitterness from her voice, but failed. "It mightn't worry *you* to lose your reputation, but it doesn't make *me* feel happy."

"You didn't have a reputation after Christopher finished talking about you," Fay said sleepily. "You heard what his brother said. He thought you were a . . . you were a. . . ." The thin face turned into the pillow and the lids were still.

Quietly Briony undressed and crept into bed. It was warm in the room yet she was shivering with cold. Every word Daniel Clayton had said returned to haunt her, reminding her of Christopher's cruel malignment. Compared with such lies, Fay's behaviour seemed far less unsavoury.

50

Fay was still lying in a drugged sleep when Briony left for the theatre next morning. She prepared a breakfast tray and left a note saying she would try to return at lunch time. "If you still feel shaky, stay in bed," she wrote. "I'm not cross with you and I'm not angry any more. I don't agree with what you did, but I understand why you did it."

Never had a morning passed with such agonising slowness and she was a mass of nerves by the time she was able to slip away from the theatre. Disregarding the cost, she took a taxi back to the flat, and as it jogged down the Strand she thought again of the way her sister had acted. Tom was right. Fay's mental state was getting worse, and unless she could be among people of her own age and not cooped up alone all day, it would deteriorate even more. The knowledge was so disturbing that she almost panicked, as though she expected Fay to turn into some strange monster, and she was shaking with nerves as she paid the taxi and ran up to the flat.

The living-room was empty and she rushed into the bedroom. "I'm back!" she cried, and stopped with a gasp as she saw Daniel Clayton by the bed. "What are *you* doing here?"

"He's come to see me," Fay spoke before the man could. Her voice was normal and the look she gave the man was warm and friendly.

Observing this and hiding her surprise, Briony came forward into the room. She was wearing the same leotard as yesterday and the black fabric clung to every curve of her figure. Devoid of make-up – as she normally was during the day – she looked considerably less than her twenty-two years and could more easily have passed for a fifteen-year-old waif, an illusion heightened by the pony-tail hair-style she adopted during practice hours. Now the thick loop of golden hair swung from side to side as she looked at Daniel Clayton.

In the daylight his skin looked paler than ever, having the milky white quality occasionally found in someone with red hair. But his hair was dark copper, and only when he stepped

51

into the light could the reddish flecks be seen. He was more formally dressed than last night, and his navy suit and white shirt marked by a plain dark tie made him look every inch the important surgeon. Angrily she stiffened.

"There was no need for you to come here personally," she said. "If you wished to enquire about my sister you could have telephoned."

"I came here to talk to you as well."

"I'm not usually home during the day," she said accusingly.

"Your sister told me you *would* be." He glanced at Fay. "I suggest you stay in bed today and rest your hip."

"Yes," Fay said meekly, and lay back against the pillows as though butter wouldn't melt in her mouth.

Silently Briony went into the sitting-room, aware of Daniel Clayton following her. He walked over to the mantelpiece and leaned against it, arms folded.

"I owe you an apology," he said abruptly. "I didn't realise how much of one until I spoke to your sister!"

Determined that this time they would not talk at cross purposes, she said: "What exactly has Fay told you?"

"She repeated what she said last night. Only more logically and with more detail."

"And the phone call to Christopher?" Briony asked.

"I don't blame you for asking for financial help," came the quiet reply.

She bit her lip hard, furious that Fay had not confessed the whole truth, for this meant that one important misconception still remained in Daniel Clayton's mind.

"I mean it," he reiterated. "I appreciate why you're disgusted with Christopher. *He's* the one who pretended. Everything he told me about you was a lie!"

"You change your mind quickly. How do you know it isn't Fay who's lying?"

"Because I'm not such a fool as I made myself look last night. Not that I'm entirely blameless. You added to it."

"In what way?"

"The way you looked." He flung up his hand. "When you opened the door to me and I saw you in that black get-up with all the muck on your face. . . ."

"I had come straight from the theatre. I often do when I'm worried about my sister."

"So she told me. But last night – seeing you like that I thought you were. . . ."

"You left me in no doubt what you thought I was," she said tartly, and was pleased to see colour seep into his cheeks. "Now you've seen me without make-up I take it you've revised your opinion of me?"

"It isn't only your lack of make-up," he admitted candidly, "but the whole flat. Last night I was too angry to notice it, but today. . . ." He glanced at the clean, shabby room, his eyes noting the carefully darned tablecloth, the sagging couch and armchair with its home-made covers in cheap chintz which did not completely hide the faded maroon velour beneath, the small black and white television set and the little bunch of copper beech carefully arranged in a white bowl: all evidence of loving care but none of it disguising the poverty. "If I had used my eyes and my own intelligence last night," he went on, "I'd have known Christopher was lying. No girl out for what she could get would need to live in a place like this!"

Appreciating the effort such an apology had cost him, Briony knew it would be churlish not to accept it. "Thank you, Mr. Clayton. Now you have made peace with yourself, I would appreciate it if you went."

"I haven't finished."

He flung out his hands and for the first time she noticed them. For someone so masculine they were surprisingly delicate-looking, with smooth palms and long, slender fingers. The hands of a violinist, she thought, and immediately corrected it. These hands held sharp instruments, and manipulated bone and muscle, not string and bow.

"Well?" she asked. "What else do you want to say?"

"How long has your sister been lame?"

The question took her by surprise and she looked at him warily. "She was born like it."

"As bad as she is now?"

"It's become worse in the last few years."

"And her hysteria?"

"There's nothing wrong with Fay's mental health. She's inclined to be excitable, that's all."

"You're talking to a doctor," he said quietly. "At the very best your sister's an hysteric in addition to whatever else is wrong with her. On the other hand that type of hysteria could be caused by – by other things."

"Christopher's behaviour didn't help her," Briony said pointedly.

"I realise that, and I regret it deeply. Please believe me."

There was such gentleness in his voice that tears blurred her eyes, and afraid he might see them she moved to the window. Framed by the light she seemed so ethereal that a breath of wind might have blown her away.

"Your sister must be a burden for you," the man continued. "The money Christopher gave you won't be enough for what you want to do."

"To do?" Briony echoed uncomprehendingly.

"For the flat you want to buy," he said. "Fay told me you're looking for something at ground level with a small garden."

Briony did not know what to say. To confess that the money was for a necklace and not a flat would mean having to tell him that Fay had been lying again. Honesty fought with loyalty and honesty won. "We don't need the –" she began, and was forcefully interrupted.

"It's obvious what you need! And it's much more than a garden flat! Your sister needs well-cooked meals and continual companionship. Not to be left cooped up here like a battery hen!"

"Battery hens aren't —"

"You know what I mean." His voice was sharp again though he had not raised it. "Wouldn't you like her to have her own suite of rooms in a well-run house? To have the best care and attention and people fussing around her?"

"I'm not sending her away from me," Briony said fiercely. "So you can forget that!"

He looked so surprised that she knew immediately she had misunderstood him. Again they seemed to be talking at cross-purposes. "What exactly are you suggesting?" she asked carefully.

"I am offering you my home. Christopher is getting married in a few weeks and I have more rooms than I need. Your sister will have the best medical care and —"

"It's impossible!" Briony said. "Anyway, Fay refuses to have any more examinations. Tom's begged her to go into hospital again, but she won't."

"I wasn't suggesting she stayed with me as a patient. My house is my home," he said with a faint smile, "not my nursing home."

"Why should you want to bother with Fay?"

He paused. "I have — I have various reasons. Partly guilt for my brother's behaviour and also because of my own."

"Forget yours," she said quickly. "I already have."

"It's very kind of you," his tone equalled hers for formality, "but it still doesn't alter the fact that if your sister lived in more congenial surroundings she would be considerably better."

The truth of this could not be denied. "If Fay's willing to stay with you I wouldn't prevent it."

"I was hoping you would come with her."

"That's out of the question. I couldn't possibly stay in your house."

"Not even as my wife?"

Convinced she had misheard him, she took a step forward. But the look on his face told her she had not made a mistake.

55

"You must be joking!"

"It's no joking matter to propose to a woman!"

"But you don't know me!"

"You are not the person I thought you were yesterday. That's the best possible recommendation!" His unexpected humour brought a faint smile to her face.

"Even so," she said breathlessly, "that's hardly a reason for marriage."

"I need a wife, Miss Stevens. I have reached a stage in my career when I need to do a great deal of entertaining. My stepmother hasn't the health to cope and it's awkward having to find women friends to act as hostess."

"I'm sure you can find someone far more suitable than me."

"I'm not looking for a normal marriage." Her raised brows drew colour into his face. "Don't misunderstand me, Miss Stevens. I was once engaged to be married and it didn't work out. After that I decided I no longer wished to concern myself with romantic love."

"I understand the feeling," she said bitterly.

"Then you can appreciate why I prefer my marriage to be purely a business arrangement." He paused and then said in a matter-of-fact tone: "The Governors of Luther Hospital have agreed to build a neurological wing, but unfortunately they can only find three-quarters of the money. I have determined to find the rest myself. That means wining and dining people whom I think might be willing to give us what we need. For that I require someone to run my home and act as hostess."

Briony's momentary liking for Daniel Clayton vanished at these words. Christopher had not told her the truth about himself, but he had certainly not been lying about his brother.

"You are ruthlessly single-minded, Mr. Clayton. You don't care whom you sacrifice in order to get the new wing."

"I'm sorry you regard it as such a sacrifice to marry me. After all, you would have an excellent social position and everything you could want for your sister."

56

"That wasn't what I meant." She saw him frown and vowed never to give him the satisfaction of knowing how easily he had forced Christopher to leave her. Yet would he have found it so easy without an invalid woman to use as leverage?

"Well?" Daniel Clayton said.

"It wouldn't work," she replied. "I'm a ballet dancer, not a society hostess."

"I'm sure you would do admirably as both."

"How can I help you with entertaining if I'm dancing at the theatre?"

"You don't dance every night. Besides, your sister has told me of the glittering future ahead of you, and where *my* charm fails to get a donation, I'm sure yours would succeed. A beautiful and famous ballerina is a jewel to be envied in anyone's crown."

Again she was shaken by disgust for his overwhelming ambition. "I could never marry you. Never!"

"Then there's no further point in discussing it. I'll leave you to tell your sister."

Without another word he walked out, closing the door quietly behind him. Briony stared after his departing back. Those red glints in his hair weren't there for nothing! And how diabolically clever his parting remark had been. "I'll leave you to tell your sister." She rubbed her hand wearily across her forehead. It required little imagination to guess what Fay's reaction would be. Suddenly the full realisation of what he had said hit her. The insufferable man must have already told Fay what he intended to do, and Fay was probably even now dreaming brighter dreams for the future. Oh no, it was impossible! He couldn't have done such a thing.

But he had. For even as she went to the bedroom the door opened and Fay peeped out, her face aglow with anticipation.

"Well, when's the wedding date?"

"There isn't going to be one," Briony stormed. "And isn't there *any* limit to what you'd do to get what you want?"

Fay's eyes filled with tears. "It isn't only for me. It's for you too. Think what it would mean if you married him. The servants – the money – the house we'd live in!"

"I'm happy here –"

"Because you're out most of the time! If you were cooped up here day after day you'd hate it as much as I do!"

Briony's heart turned over and her anger was replaced by compassion. "I know what it would mean to you if we could move out, but I still can't do it."

"Why not? Think how Christopher would feel if you did!"

This was something Briony had not thought about until now, and she could not help wondering what his reaction would be if she were presented to him as his sister-in-law. Although he had professed to love her, he had been able to walk out of her life and – far more heinous – had preferred to ruin *her* name rather than admit his own deception. The knowledge made her despise not only him, but also herself for not having recognised the weakness of his character. Never again would she let herself fall in love. Ballet was her life and nothing else mattered. Of course if she did not have to worry about Fay's welfare. . . . But no, it was impossible.

"I can't marry Daniel Clayton," she reiterated. "He's inhuman!"

"Well, it's your choice," Fay mumbled, and turned back to the bedroom. Her foot caught in the frayed edge of the carpet and she toppled and fell.

Instantly Briony was at her side, lifting her up. "You're right, Fay," she said fiercely. "We can't go on living in a dump like this. If we don't get out of this flat soon. . . . I *will* marry Mr. Clayton."

"Oh, Briony!" The thin face was alight with happiness. "I know you're doing the right thing."

"I hope it will be the right thing for *you*," Briony said. "That's the only reason I'm doing it. At least *someone's* dreams will come true!"

# CHAPTER FIVE

If Daniel Clayton was surprised to receive Briony's telephone call saying she had changed her mind and was willing to be his wife, he gave no sign of it. It was the first time she had spoken to him on the telephone, and his disembodied voice gave no indication of his character or looks. Calm and quiet, it yet had a reassuring quality which she found surprising until she remembered it was part of his professional repertoire.

With a start she realised he was asking her if she would be prepared to marry him at once.

"Now we have made up our minds, there is no point delaying it."

"What you really mean is that you want to make sure *Christopher* doesn't have a chance of changing his mind!" she retorted.

There was such a long silence that she was not sure he was still on the line, and was about to speak again when he finally did so.

"I won't bother taking that remark seriously. I'll call round and see you tonight."

"I'm dancing."

"I'll pick you up at the theatre, then."

That night Briony was dancing the role of the Sugar Plum Fairy in *The Nutcracker*. The acceptance of Daniel Clayton's offer of marriage unexpectedly lightened her mood, as though she were already sharing the burden of Fay with a more competent person than herself, and she gave the role a lightness she had never before achieved, drawing a spontaneous ovation at the end.

"Now you have stopped worrying about the necklace," Oleg Beloff greeted her as she came breathlessly into the wings, "you are dancing with your heart as well as your head."

Thought of the necklace had been so far from Briony's mind that it took several seconds for the remark to register, and when it did she hastily nodded. Time enough to tell the director what she had done when she was already married.

Nervous of the meeting ahead of her, she carefully prepared herself for it, unable to stop a slight smile at the memory of how she must have looked when Daniel Clayton had first seen her. Tonight her face was pale and shiny, and she decided to armour herself with a little sophistication, thickening her lashes with mascara and outlining the delicate curve of her mouth with lipstick. Only as she slipped on a plain black dress did she regret not having something more feminine to wear. Not that it mattered what she looked like so long as she was presentable. Time enough to act the society hostess when she had become one. The idea was so frightening that she flung her coat over her shoulders and ran to the stage door.

A few people were standing there with autograph books, but they were waiting for the stars and did not recognise the pale, slim girl as the exotic creature they had applauded earlier. Hesitantly she stepped out into the darkness and as the damp November air billowed around her she shivered and went to put her arms into the sleeves of her coat. As she did so it was lifted from her shoulders and held up for her.

"You should have put it on before you came out," Daniel Clayton said behind her, and came round to stand in her path. He appeared so calm and unruffled that her nervousness evaporated, disappearing completely as he took her elbow and guided her along the pavement.

"My car's parked at the end of the road."

"I don't mind a walk."

"I thought you'd be tired after your performance tonight."

"That was a rest cure! Our practice during the day is far harder than that."

"No wonder you're thin!"

60

"I'm all muscle."

Unexpectedly he caught the tip of her arm and squeezed it.

"Ouch!" she cried. "You needn't take me so literally!"

"I'm a literal person – by instinct and training."

"Then I'll have to mind what I say to you."

"For the next few months we will both have to mind what we say." He was suddenly serious. "Marriage is never easy."

"It's probably easier when two people aren't in love with each other," she replied. "We can at least behave normally without the usual sexual hang-ups."

"I hadn't thought of it in those terms," he said gravely, and stopped beside a black limousine.

It was the sort of car she had expected him to have, the sliding glass partition indicating that it was normally driven by a chauffeur.

Interpreting her glance correctly he said: "I gave Marriot the night off. I don't keep him late unless I have to operate."

"I thought only gynaecologists were called out at night!"

"Sometimes there are accidents. Concussion can lead to brain damage."

All the time they had been talking he had been driving, but so skilfully – and with none of Christopher's dash – that they had stopped outside a restaurant before she was aware of it.

"You were supposed to be taking me home," she accused. "Fay –"

"Knows I'm taking you out. Stop arguing."

Silently Briony preceded him into a dimly lit foyer. Again he was different from Christopher, choosing a sombre restaurant in place of a swinging discotheque. But the long room with its small tables and shining cutlery looked expensively simple, and the food when it came was excellent and French. His choice of wine complemented the meal, being a delicate claret with a fine bouquet.

"You can't go wrong with this vintage," he said as she sipped appreciatively.

"I could go wrong with anything," she admitted. "I'm not a gourmet."

"You have had no chance to be. I'm sure you'll learn when you have the opportunity."

"Will that be part of my duty?" she asked, bringing the conversation back to the reason for their *tête-à-tête*.

"Yes," he said. "But for the first few months my step-mother will continue to supervise my home."

He spoke with an assurance that irritated her, though she had to concede that it enabled him to invest this embarrassing discussion with a detachment that robbed it of anything personal.

Only when coffee was set before them did he appear to relax a little. "You're a beautiful dancer, Briony."

It was his first use of her name and her heart thumped. But she kept her expression casual. "If I'd known you were coming to the performance I'd have got you a ticket."

"It wasn't until the last minute that I knew I could make it. I was operating late and only got to the theatre as the curtain went up."

"I hope you got a decent seat."

"I had to stand."

She was astonished that he had wanted to see her dance sufficiently to do this.

"I can see why my brother fell in love with you," he went on. "Though how he was persuaded to go to the ballet in the first place . . ."

"We met at my flat," she said bluntly. "He's an old school friend of Tom Bristow – our doctor."

"I see." Daniel Clayton poured some more coffee.

Even the mellow glow of the restaurant failed to give warmth to his skin, though it added more red to his hair. He wore it longer than she had expected, and though it stopped well short of his collar it was still thick on the back of his neck.

"Do you think we're wise to get married?" she asked impulsively.

"Certainly. We are both marrying for logical reasons that have nothing to do with the insanity of love."

The coldness of his reply left her at a loss, and as if aware of it he leaned across the table.

"Don't be scared, Briony. We're both doing the best thing." He stopped and smiled. "Which reminds me, you haven't yet used *my* name. After tomorrow you can't very well go on calling me Mr. Clayton."

"Why after tomorrow?"

"That's when we're getting married."

This time she could not hide her astonishment, and he laughed. It was the first time he had done so and it made a marked difference to his expression, lightening his face so that he seemed less than the thirty-five she knew him to be.

"Why so soon?" she gasped. "I haven't got a –"

"Thing to wear!" he finished for her. "You wouldn't have even if we waited a month! No, my dear, I'm a great believer in Macbeth's philosophy. 'If it were done when 'tis done, then t'were well it were done quickly.' And there's no point in our waiting."

"Of course not," she murmured, and pushed her coffee cup away from her.

"You're tired," he said abruptly, and signalled for the bill.

Only as they drove back to the flat did she ask him whether Christopher knew they were getting married.

"No one knows," he replied. "I intend to tell Sylvie – my stepmother – in the morning."

"How will she feel about your marrying the girl Christopher –"

"She won't know it was you. My brother never told her your name."

Emotion made it impossible for Briony to reply, and she stared unseeingly through the window.

"You still love him, don't you?" Daniel Clayton went on. "I'm sorry he hurt you so badly."

They reached her block of flats and he stopped the car and stepped out to open the door for her. "Say goodnight to your sister for me, and tell her I'm looking forward to seeing her tomorrow."

Only then was Briony able to speak. "Do you — do you want Fay there when we — when we —"

"Of course. It's at noon at Caxton Hall. I'll send Marriot for you."

"There's no need to bother."

"It's no bother. Besides, in less than twelve hours from now he'll be *your* chauffeur too!"

There was no doubting she was being teased, and with an effort she smiled.

"That's better," he said gravely. "I don't want you to get cold feet."

"As a dancer my circulation's too good," she said, and watching him drive away was glad she had managed to make her last remark a humorous one.

Looking back on the simple wedding ceremony that made her Daniel Clayton's wife, Briony could remember only one thing clearly: her sister's delight. Anyone seeing the two girls as they came out of Caxton Hall would have supposed Fay to be the bride.

They lunched at the Ritz, and staring at the diamond ring encircling her finger, Briony realised that from now on she could afford to come to places like this by herself. Somehow the thought held no pleasure. Yet why should it? She had wanted money in order to improve Fay's life, not her own. But to obtain this she had been obliged to give up her freedom, and from this moment on must share her life with a man who was a total stranger to her.

Surreptitiously she watched him. In Fay's presence he seemed more light-hearted than the night before. Perhaps he was not at such ease with her as he pretended to be? He might speak glibly of his need for a hostess to help him scale the ambitious heights he had set himself, but this did not mean he had not found it an effort to take the fatal step of marriage.

Marriage. The word made her shiver. Surely if things didn't work out he would not hold her to bond? When he had achieved the neurological wing *he* might even decide he no longer needed a wife. What would happen then? Could he as a surgeon risk his reputation by divorce? Yet today a divorce would not even cause a ripple on the pool of social convention.

"You seem very pensive, Briony!"

The calmness of Daniel Clayton's voice made her realise the irrationality of her thoughts and she pushed them to the back of her mind and turned her attention to Fay. The girl looked almost pretty in a beige woollen dress which, though several years old, was simple enough in style not to have dated. She had made an effort to style her hair, and instead of wearing it straight had coiled it into a chignon. Tendrils kept escaping, but it nonetheless softened the sharp bones of her face. A face that was far too thin and pain-racked for beauty, Briony felt, and bit back a sigh. If only Daniel Clayton was right in believing that proper care and attention would make Fay considerably better. It was odd that a surgeon should have expressed an opinion she would have expected from a psychologist. But then Daniel Clayton – she really must start thinking of him by his first name only – was an unusual man; even her short acquaintance with him had told her that.

"I never thought the Ritz was so gay," Fay said, clutching her sister's arm and looking round the room.

Following her sister's gaze Briony noticed how spring-like the restaurant was, despite the dullness of the November day. It must come from the profusion of flowers and the pale green walls.

"What did Beloff say when you told him you were getting married?" Fay asked suddenly.

"I daren't repeat the exact words!" Briony smiled, remembering the director's explosive fury which had only abated when she had assured him that far from decreasing her dedication to her work, marriage would enable her to devote more time to it.

"I'd never have the perseverance to be a ballet dancer," Fay said to Daniel. "Even when you reach the top you can't sit back and relax."

He set down his fork and looked at Briony. "Have *you* ever regretted it?"

"Never. It's as much a part of my life as breathing."

"Have *you* regretted being a neurological surgeon?" Fay posed the question which Briony had been reluctant to ask.

Daniel shook his head. "Ever since I can remember, it was my only ambition. But unlike dancing, it isn't a question of practice leading to perfection."

"Surely surgeons improve?" Briony asked, in surprise.

"Only up to a point. Neuro-surgery requires delicate precision work, and of course the ability to do that is a gift." He flexed his hands, their long elegance striking compared with his broad shoulders. A watch glinted gold on his wrist, and glancing at it, he frowned. "I don't like rushing you both, but I have to be back at the hospital by three."

"On your wedding day?" Fay expostulated.

Colour flooded Briony's face. Sometimes she wondered whether her sister was naïve or mischievous. "You know very well our marriage is a business arrangement," she said clearly. "There's no need to pretend about it."

"I'm glad Fay said what she did," Daniel interposed. "It's something I'd like to discuss with you."

"If you want to talk to Briony alone," Fay said, "I can go and powder my nose."

"I'd like you to hear it too. After all," he said pointedly, "you were partly the reason for our marriage."

He looked at Briony again, his eyes more green than she had remembered them. If it were not for the eyes it would be difficult to know he was related to Christopher, for his colouring was so different, as were his features. They were stronger: the chin square and determined, the mouth wide and thin.

"As far as other people are concerned," he continued, "I'd prefer them to think our marriage is a normal one. There'll be enough gossip at the suddenness of it without adding to it by disclosing the real reason."

Briony appreciated the argument. He certainly wouldn't want anyone to know he had taken a wife in order to further his ambitious plans, nor that he had chosen her because her own career would – as he had so aptly put it – be "an additional diamond in anyone's crown."

"Naturally we'll have adjoining rooms," he added. "I wasn't suggesting we pretend beyond the bedroom door!"

Briony went scarlet, but Fay took the remark in her stride and said: "Won't that make your servants gossip?"

"Not at all. Briony and I each have our work, and it's more practical to have separate rooms. When I operate I like to be at the hospital at seven in the morning, and I frequently go back at night to see a patient."

"You both work in a theatre," Fay said inconsequentially. "Yet you do entirely different things."

"They each have their own value," he said.

"But yours is far greater."

"It's equally important to give pleasure to people."

"There's no joy without health," Fay said. "No one knows that better than me."

"One day you may have both," Daniel replied.

"I'm not going to let any more doctors mess about with me!"

"The choice is yours, my dear." He pushed back his chair and looked at Briony. "I'd like to take you home before I go to Luther's. My stepmother is anxious to meet you."

It was not until they were sitting in the back of the car that Briony asked him where they were supposed to have met.

"At the theatre," he said. "I fell in love with your dancing and sent you a note back-stage."

"That doesn't sound in character with you!"

"I'm considered a law unto myself."

His voice was unexpectedly cool and she was glad she was not one of the nurses working under him; so would he speak to anyone who did not meet his high demands.

"Are you quite sure your stepmother won't suspect who I am? I mean, Christopher said the girl *he* knew was a dancer?"

"He told Sylvie you were a chorus girl."

The words twisted in Briony like a serrated knife and she clenched her hands and fought for composure. The uncomfortable feel of the wedding ring biting into her flesh made her relax. She must not let the knowledge of Christopher's treachery affect her like this. She was now his half-brother's wife: as far out of his reach as he had been out of hers.

"We're nearly home," Daniel murmured, and only then did she see they were driving in Regent's Park.

"Where's your house?" she asked.

"Cumberland Terrace. It was my father's home, but when he died I made extensive alterations."

The car swung out of the main park road and into a narrow crescent lined with graceful Nash houses, stopping as it reached a double-fronted one at the end. It had cream walls and several steps led up to a shiny black door. The lower windows were decorated by boxes filled with green shrubs, but there was nothing else to mar the simple lines of the house.

"Marriot will bring the cases," Daniel said, and ushered Briony and Fay into a narrow hall lined with doors. Facing them a well-proportioned staircase led to the first floor.

"Can I go straight to *my* room?" Fay asked, looking suddenly pale.

"Certainly," he replied, and moved over to a wrought-iron door. Only as he opened it did they realise it was a lift.

"It's very small," Fay said doubtfully. "Is it safe?"

"Of course. I had it installed after my stepmother's heart attack."

There was just room for the three of them in it, and in the confined space Daniel seemed overbearingly large. He looked more like a rugger player than a surgeon, Briony decided, and could see him controlling a team of men as easily as he did the operating theatre. No wonder his father had left the business to him instead of Christopher! The thought took her by surprise, and she was still analysing it when the lift stopped and they stepped on to a small landing, close-carpeted in beige. Here there were two doors, each leading to a large bedroom-cum-sitting-room, and each with its own bathroom.

"Fay and Sylvie will share this floor," Daniel said to Briony, "and you and I have the one below."

"Where does Christopher live?" Briony asked with icy calm.

"At the top of the house. I turned it into a self-contained flat for him. He'll be moving out once he's married – as I told you."

"It would make ideal nursery quarters!" Fay put in.

"Fay!" Briony burst out angrily.

"Don't let your sister embarrass you," Daniel said dryly. "What she said is true, anyway. They'd make an ideal nursery suite." He stopped and opened the door on his left, and Fay stepped ahead of him, exclaiming with delight as she saw the beautiful room that was to be her own. It ran the depth of the house, on one side facing Regent's Park which, even in mid-winter, presented a picture of tranquil calm, and on the other a quiet mews. Here there was a balcony with table and chairs and several tubs which, though only filled with earth, gave promise of colour to come. This part of the room held easy chairs, a desk and television and hi-fi set. There was even a pile of new magazines on a table, and Briony marvelled that the man standing so phlegmatically beside her had had the forethought to have this room so painstakingly prepared. How sure he had been that she would accept his strange proposal of marriage!

Leaving Fay ecstatically purring over every item, Daniel led Briony down to the next floor, murmured: "Our rooms," and then proceeded to a lower floor still.

Briony would have liked a chance to tidy herself before meeting Mrs. Clayton, but Daniel was already halfway into the drawing-room. She had a swift impression of velvet settees and armchairs, silk Persian rugs gleaming on a highly polished floor and small Regency tables covered with bowls of flowers and silver-framed photographs, before she found herself grasped by the elbow and led over to the woman lying on a lemon brocade couch. Her relationship to Christopher was obvious, for she had the same blonde hair and Grecian features. But in close-up the blondeness was streaked with grey, and there were a myriad lines around the eyes and mouth.

"So you're the girl who finally captured Daniel! Welcome into our family, my dear."

Briony was caught by unexpectedly strong hands and clasped in a warm embrace. As she stepped back, Daniel put an arm casually over her shoulders.

"Well, Sylvie," he said, "what do you think of my bride?"

Brown eyes regarded them both, then rested on Briony. As though reassured by what she saw, the woman relaxed against the cushions.

"She is very much like your own mother," came the soft reply.

Though Daniel did not move, Briony was aware of him tensing, for held close against his side she felt his muscles harden. But when he spoke his voice was as calm as always.

"You are the only mother I remember, Sylvie."

"Consciously perhaps, but you were four when your own

mother died, so you must have *some* memory of her." Mrs. Clayton smiled at Briony. "The day I met my late husband he showed me photographs of his first wife. He was determined not to let me be jealous of a ghost. But you *are* like Daniel's mother. You have the same colouring and expression."

She patted the settee beside her and, afraid of the catechism to follow but not knowing how to avoid it, Briony sat down.

"I'll leave you both to get acquainted," Daniel said. "I must get back to Luther's." He bent over Briony and kissed her brow.

The touch was brief, but it left her trembling, and she had to force herself to concentrate on what Mrs. Clayton was saying.

"I really should be cross with Daniel for keeping his marriage a secret. But he said he did it because he didn't want me to get excited, especially with Christopher going to have such a big wedding." She half-smiled. "Mind you, I knew Daniel was excited about *something* these last couple of days. He went around looking shattered."

It was not an adjective Briony would have applied to him, but his stepmother repeated it, smiling as she said: "I bet it was only yesterday that he asked you to marry him?"

"It was, as a matter of fact."

"And if I know Daniel, he produced the licence the minute you said yes!"

Since this was exactly what had happened, Briony nodded. "Is he always so impetuous?"

"If he's sure in his own mind, and he obviously was, as far as you were concerned."

"And here I am – thrust on you like a parcel," Briony apologised. "I'll try not to interfere in anything and –"

"My dear girl," Mrs. Clayton interrupted, "this is *your* home, not mine. I'm only here because Daniel lets me stay, but I'd be perfectly happy to move out."

"Oh, you mustn't. Not on my account."

"Daniel told me you'd say that." Only the sigh which accompanied the words gave indication of worry. "He's been like a son to me, you know. Sometimes I feel closer to him than I do to Christopher. Even though they had the same father, they're quite different in temperament. Christopher has lots of charm but no staying power, and Daniel doesn't bother with charm at all – except where his patients are concerned – though he's exceptionally kind underneath. As I'm sure you know," she added.

"I don't," Briony said. "I – I haven't known Daniel very long. Our marriage was – was rather sudden."

"All the more romantic! I've been so afraid he'd never marry after his –" Mrs. Clayton stopped abruptly, her skilfully applied make-up standing out in blotches on her face. "My pills," she gasped. "They're on the table by the window." She waited, her breath shallow, while Briony found the pills, filled a glass from a carafe of water and gave it to her. "I'll be better in a moment," she murmured, swallowing them. "It's the excitement of seeing you."

"I'll leave you to rest for a while," said Briony. "I have my unpacking to do anyway."

But once on the landing she was reluctant to go to her room, and on an impulse decided to look at the rest of the house.

As she had anticipated, the dining-room was formal, with Hepplewhite furniture set against white walls and several softly lit alcoves holding exquisite Chinese porcelain. Beyond it was a butler's pantry with a dumb waiter which, she surmised, led down to the kitchen, while on the left was a breakfast room, brightly furnished with bamboo and chintz. Here French windows gave on to a gay tiled patio which, even on this dull November day, brought Italy vividly to mind.

Back in the hall again there was only one room left to see, and she paused outside its doors, certain it was Daniel's private sanctum. Drawing a deep breath, she turned the handle. No other room so clearly epitomised his character as this one did. Dark green carpet covered the floor, its sombreness relieved by several Bokhara rugs, their strong colours so different from the delicate silk prayer rugs in the drawing room above. The furniture here was black and warm brown leather: modern Italian chairs that swung round at the lightest touch. Only the one behind the desk was more stolid; a battered wing chair that spoke of many years' usage. Far more than Daniel could have given it, she decided, and instinctively guessed it had belonged to his father, as did the heavy mahogany desk. It was a surprising touch of sentiment to find in a man she had suspected of having none and, made curious by it, she wandered round the room. There were many signed photographs of celebrities and Royalty, each one indicating the fame of the man who was now her husband, and making his ambition to have his own neurological wing more understandable.

She was thinking of this as she stepped into the hall, and did not notice that the front door had opened until she caught sight of a tall blond figure through the ribbed glass door of the vestibule. With a gasp she went to go back into the library, but her hand was wet with perspiration and her fingers slipped on the knob. Before she could grasp it again the man stepped into the hall, staring at her as though he had seen a ghost.

"Briony!" Christopher whispered, and turned an unbecoming yellow. "What are – why are you. . . ."

"Hullo, Christopher," she said huskily. "You're just in time to congratulate me."

"Congratulate you? Why?"

"I've married your brother."

In the silence that followed every sound was magnified: the hum of traffic from the park; the whining of the lift as it moved from one floor to the other; the ticking of the beautiful grandfather clock that stood in the well of the stairs.

"If this is your idea of a joke –" Christopher said angrily.

"It's no joke. It's true."

"You're lying!" He caught her shoulder and pushed her into the library, closing the door firmly behind him and lean-

73

ing on it as though afraid she would run out. "Now then, what's it all about? I gave Fay every penny I could lay my hands on. I can't give you any more even if I wanted to. For God's sake, Briony, don't destroy me!"

"Be quiet!" she cried. "Don't make me despise you more than I do already. I knew nothing of Fay's call until after he'd spoken to you. I was horrified when I found out."

"You didn't return the money!"

"How could I? She had already given it to Mr. Van der Heim."

Christopher's eyes narrowed. "You mean it's true about the necklace?"

"Of course it's true! She was desperate to help me. That's why she rang you and made those stupid threats. If you don't believe me, ring Mr. Van der Heim yourself. We still owe him five hundred pounds."

"I can't raise another penny," Christopher retorted. "Not for at least several months."

"I haven't asked you to," she said sharply. "What Fay did was unforgivable. Neither of us would have told your mother or your fiancée about –" Briony clenched her hands. "It was a pity you had so little faith in me. If you had rung me after you'd spoken to Fay you'd have saved yourself the money."

"You needed it anyway," he muttered.

"Mr. Beloff was going to help me," Briony said.

"That still doesn't explain how you and Daniel.... You were joking, weren't you?"

"No. I *am* his wife."

"I can't believe it!"

Christopher ran his hands through his hair, tousling the thick blond strands and making her long to reach out and smooth them. With an effort she remained where she was: she no longer had the right to make any gesture of warmth to him.

"Why?" he asked unexpectedly. "Don't tell me you fell in love with each other?"

74

"Why should that surprise you? *You* said you fell in love with me when you first saw me."

"That was different. I'm more susceptible than Daniel."

Christopher pursed his lips, and looking at him Briony had to resist the urge to lash out at him. How arrogant and unfeeling he was! And how cunningly he had lied to her. The few moments she had seen Daniel spend with Mrs. Clayton had clearly shown her *that*. Daniel might be determined that Christopher should marry Maureen, but she was certain he would never use his stepmother as a lever. No, Christopher had made up that part of the story to suit his own ends. Daniel undoubtedly had *other* ways of putting on the pressure. But for the moment she was too disturbed by Christopher's presence to think what these could be.

"You haven't answered me," Christopher reminded her. "Are you and Daniel in love, or did he marry you to make sure *I* wouldn't!"

It was a logical assumption in the circumstances, and Briony wondered why it annoyed her. "Why don't you ask Daniel yourself?"

"I might do that." Colour had returned to Christopher's face and he looked more in command of himself. "Where's Fay?"

"Staying here."

"I bet that pleases her!"

"Naturally. After the flat, *anything* would be heaven."

Too late Briony realised she had given herself away, for Christopher's expression lightened. No longer in a state of shock, his normal intelligence had returned and he instantly pounced on the remark. "You married Daniel to give Fay a home, didn't you? And to get your own back on *me*!"

"*You* had nothing to do with it. It was because of Fay. If it hadn't been for her I wouldn't have wanted to see you *or* your brother again! But she's ill, as you know – and – your behaviour didn't help her any."

75

"I'm sorry about that." He looked uncomfortable. "I had no idea she took everything I said so seriously."

"Didn't you think I took it seriously either?"

"You know why I had to leave you," he burst out.

"You gave me a reason," she said quietly, "but I don't believe it any more – not after seeing Daniel with your mother. He'd never do anything to hurt her."

Christopher's colour returned with a rush. "He can hurt *me*. And that would hurt my mother. My father's will put him in a position of power and he wouldn't hesitate to use it if I didn't do what he wanted." The blond head tilted nervously. "That reminds me, Maureen is dining here tonight. But if you and Daniel are on your honeymoon –" he stopped. "Or aren't you having one?"

"I can't get away from the theatre and –"

"He can't get away from the hospital! Not that there'd be much point in either of you getting away," Christopher said, grinning maliciously.

Belatedly she remembered Daniel had asked her to pretend their marriage was a normal one. But surely he hadn't been thinking of Christopher when he had said it? Anyway, it was too late to pretend now.

"Daniel doesn't want anyone to know that our marriage isn't normal."

"I'm not surprised. He really *is* determined to let nothing prevent him having that new wing, isn't he? As long as you were free he'd have been scared I'd break off with Maureen."

"You're getting married in a month," she said pointedly.

"A month can be a long time if you're worried," Christopher replied. "And my estimable brother was very worried indeed. But as always he grasped the nettle with both hands – if you'll forgive me calling you a nettle!"

"You're despicable," she flared.

"I know. But so is Daniel. Don't forget that, Briony. You'll get even more hurt if you do."

# CHAPTER SIX

CHANGING for dinner that night into the plain black silk she had worn when Christopher had taken her to the Savoy, Briony realised how shabby all her clothes were. Only the grace of her body made this one anywhere near presentable. The wealthy Maureen would no doubt be couturier dressed!

Pushing aside the unwelcome thought, she ran down to the drawing room, where Fay was already talking to Mrs. Clayton.

"I hope you don't mind, Briony, but I came down and introduced myself," her sister said cheerily.

Briony felt uneasy, but as she watched Fay talk her uneasiness died. The girl looked calmer than she had done for a long time, her body resting easily in the chair instead of poised nervously on the edge of it.

Mrs. Clayton, in a long pastel-coloured dress, was explaining her daily routine. "I either go down for lunch or dinner. Daniel won't let me sit up for both meals. But tonight I'm breaking his rule. After all, he doesn't get married every day!"

"I should hope not," Fay giggled. "He didn't strike me as a Bluebeard!"

"He's anything but. Daniel's trouble is that he's too faithful."

"That sounds as though he's been in love before."

A nervous look crossed Mrs. Clayton's face, and realising she had said too much she switched the conversation. It was just in time, for at that moment Christopher came in with a dark-haired girl.

Maureen was not at all the way Briony had imagined her, being candid of face and boyish of figure, with an outspoken friendliness that was immediately warming. She looked as if she would be more at home in the country surrounded by dogs and children than in the bright lights her future husband preferred, and as Christopher served the drinks, she confided to Briony that this was her intention. They would live in a flat for the first few months they were married, but Christopher had already designed the house they were going to build on the two acres of land which her father had given to them on his estate in Sussex.

Each word was like a stab in Briony's heart, and she almost cried with relief as a door slammed and Mrs. Clayton looked at her.

"Daniel's back, my dear."

Doing what was expected of her, Briony hurried from the room, and was halfway down the stairs when Daniel looked up and saw her.

"The loving wife rushing to greet her husband!"

"It's what you ordered," she reminded him. "I'm quite willing to stop the pretence."

"Not at all." He looked apologetic. "I wasn't being rude. I meant it as a joke."

She shrugged, watching silently as he dropped his overcoat on to a chair. He looked tired, his pale skin faintly grey around the mouth, and she realised that while she had been resting for the afternoon, he had been working.

"Were you busy at the hospital?" she asked.

"Yes. But not with patients. I had to get back to Luther's for a Governors' Meeting. We were discussing the new wing."

Her sympathy disappeared as his words reminded her of the reason he had wanted their marriage, and seeing her expression, his own hardened.

"What's wrong, Briony? You look as if you could kill me!"

"I feel I could." She paused. "I've just seen Christopher. He made me see how cunning you are. Now I'm married to *you*, he couldn't marry me even if he left Maureen!"

"You knew that would be the case when you accepted my

78

proposal," Daniel said. "But even if we *weren't* married, Christopher wouldn't return to you."

"How can you be so sure?" Her eyes blazed. "What hold do you have over him? What threats are you using? I know it can't be your stepmother."

"You know so much, Briony, that you've forgotten the reasons *I* gave you for our marriage. But I would like to remind you that they still exist. I need a hostess and you need help with Fay." He walked across to the lift and held open the door for her.

"I suggest you wait with me while I change," he continued, as they glided upwards. "It will look better if we go into the drawing room together."

"Why pretend in your own home?" she burst out. "Christopher knows the truth!"

Daniel swung round so sharply that he almost knocked her over. "I told you not to tell anyone!"

"I didn't mean to," she admitted. "He guessed."

"You haven't said anything to Sylvie or Maureen?"

"No."

"Then don't."

There was so much menace in his voice that she shivered. The last time he had spoken to her in that tone she had been free to tell him to go out of her life. But now she was his wife, legally joined to him.

The thought filled her with disquiet as she nervously waited for him in her bedroom. Through the closed door she heard drawers opening and closing, then the splash of running water and an expletive as though something had been dropped. They were the familiar sounds of a man changing and they carried her back down the years to when her father had been alive. But he was alive no longer, and the burden of Fay was solely hers. That was why she had married Daniel. As long as she remembered this, she would be able to make the marriage work.

*

More quickly than she had anticipated, Briony settled down to life in Cumberland Terrace. Only her meetings with Christopher remained a source of unhappiness and she tried to avoid him as much as possible. It was easy when she was dancing at the theatre, for on her return she went straight to her room, where a supper tray was always waiting for her. But on the evenings when she was free she was forced to sit at the dinner table with him, and frequently with Maureen too, listening to the girl's chatter about her forthcoming marriage and their honeymoon in the Bahamas.

"When are you and Daniel going away?" Maureen asked one evening.

"Neither Briony nor I can leave our work at the moment," Daniel said, while Briony was still searching for an answer.

"How unromantic you are, Daniel," Maureen teased. "If I were your wife I wouldn't stand for it."

"That's why you're not my wife!"

Maureen grinned at Briony. "Don't you mind not having a honeymoon?"

Once again Briony was forestalled, this time by Fay.

"Beloff's doing a new ballet for her, so she *has* to be around all the time."

Briony flashed her sister a furious look, wishing she had had the foresight to swear her to secrecy before telling her the news.

"A new ballet for you?" Daniel came into the conversation gently but firmly. "Why didn't you tell me before, darling?"

"I wanted it to be a surprise for you," she said quickly.

"What's the story?"

"A Greek legend. It's rather sentimental and romantic."

"Just the part Briony will dance perfectly," Fay enthused. "A fisherman drowns and a mermaid finds his body and falls in love with him. She begs the gods to bring him to life again and agrees to forfeit her own life instead."

"You should dance the part to perfection," Daniel murmured. "A girl sacrificing everything for love."

Stormily Briony met his eyes, but there was a softness in them that told her he had not been sarcastic, and surprised by this, she looked unwilling for anything to disturb her dislike of him.

"It sounds too schmaltzy for me," said Christopher. "You should dance modern ballet."

"No, she shouldn't." Daniel interposed, and stared at Briony again. "I saw you in *Daphnis and Chloe* last night, and you were perfect."

Once more he had surprised her, and this time she could not hide it. "I only took over the part at the last moment. How did you find out?"

"I've made arrangements to be told when you're dancing solo."

"Why can't Briony tell you herself?" Mrs. Clayton asked.

"Because she's still too shy of me. She insists on hiding her talents!"

"You never told me you took over Davina's role," Fay said.

"It was pure chance," Briony tried to mask her embarrassment. "Davina got food poisoning and Beloff couldn't find a replacement."

"No one could have danced it better than you," Daniel repeated.

"Is that spoken as a loving husband," Christopher asked, "or as a critical balletomane?"

"Both!"

"All this talk of dancing," Mrs. Clayton commented, "and I haven't even seen Briony hop!"

"I'll let you know when I'm dancing the Lilac Fairy again," Briony promised.

"Spare me from *that*," said Christopher.

"You weren't being invited," Briony retorted.

"That's put you in your place, my darling," Maureen said to him, and caught hold of his hand.

It was one of many gestures of affection which she displayed towards him, and as always he flashed Briony a look of apprehension.

"Only another week to the wedding," Maureen continued. "I'm so excited!"

"At least you're giving us the chance to dress up," Mrs. Clayton said. "That's more than Daniel did!"

"Perhaps Daniel will give us an occasion in the future," Christopher said in a mocking tone. "A christening, perhaps!"

Briony was glad she had no food in her mouth, for she would have choked on it. How dare Christopher talk like this when he knew what a mockery her marriage was: a mockery because she still loved *him*. Desperately she wondered if she could plead tiredness immediately dinner was over and go to bed, but fearing this would draw even more embarrassing remarks from him, she knew she would have to sit it out.

But in this she had under-estimated Daniel, for as they left the dining room he asked her to come with him to the library.

"I have some papers to look through, but it will relax me if I can look up and see you."

Aware of the surprised look on Christopher's face, Briony followed Daniel out.

Her belief that she would only need to stay in the library until everyone had settled themselves in the drawing room and she could retire to her bedroom without being seen was shattered by Daniel sitting opposite her in front of the fire and giving every indication of wishing to talk.

"I'm too tired to work," he explained. "So you can keep me company instead."

"What sort of work do you usually do in here?" she asked.

"Reading mainly. I like to keep up with the latest techniques, and that means reading the medical journals. Then of course I'm often asked to write articles myself."

"You work hard," she commented.

82

"So do you."

"My work isn't as valuable as yours."

"We seem to have had this conversation before," he said dryly.

"Do you remember everything we've said?"

"If I think it's important." There was a pause. "I like your taste in clothes. Your new dresses are very becoming."

"You make it easy for me," she smiled. "Your allowance is more than generous."

"I can afford it." He stood up and walked around the room. For such a well-built man he moved quietly and quickly. It was at variance with his slow but incisive way of speaking, and she wondered what he was like in the hospital. A martinet, if Christopher was to be believed.

"I'd like you to buy something special for Christopher's wedding." Daniel's voice made her start with surprise. "I put a thousand pounds in your account this morning."

"For one dress?" she exclaimed.

"You'll need a fur as well. A mink jacket, I think. The pale blonde colour. It will go with your hair." He pointed to the honey-gold cloud that fell around her shoulders. "You should always wear it loose. It suits you."

The words were an echo of Christopher's, and she clenched her hands. "I'd cut it short if I could."

"I'd spank you if you did."

She went scarlet and stared fixedly at the fire.

"Fay is walking quite well," he said unexpectedly.

This was safe ground as a topic and Briony responded to it. "That's because she's relaxed. When she's depressed it always affects her walking."

"Have her changes of mood always done that?"

"I'm not sure. She never used to be moody at all – she was the exact opposite, in fact. It's only in the last few years that she's started getting headaches and it – it sort of developed from there."

"Would you object if I spoke to her doctor?"

"Not at all. But it won't do any good. She says she'll never go into hospital again, and I won't let you force her."

"I've no intention of forcing her. I'd merely like to talk to her doctor. You told me he's a friend of yours, so it wouldn't be unusual if you were to invite him here to dinner. I'm sure he'd welcome the chance of seeing you."

Briony was annoyed for not having thought of the idea herself. How rude Tom must think her. He might even believe that now she was married to Daniel Clayton she no longer had any need of him. The thought of Tom's stocky figure and freckled face filled her with a longing to see him and apologise for her silence.

"I'll see if he's free for dinner tomorrow," she said. "I'm not dancing and it's the one night he doesn't do surgery."

"Good. Why not ring him now?"

Conscious of him watching her, she dialled Tom's number. He was at home and delighted to accept her invitation. She knew Fay had spoken to him recently, but this was the first time she herself had done so since her marriage.

"I'm looking forward to meeting your husband," he said. "He's a brilliant surgeon."

"You must tell him so yourself."

"Doctors don't talk to each other in eulogistic terms. We're not members of the theatrical profession!"

She was still smiling at the remark as she put down the telephone, and turning, was surprised to find Daniel directly behind her, so close that she could smell the shaving lotion he used.

"Tom will come tomorrow," she said breathlessly.

"Excellent." Daniel put up a hand and tilted her chin so that she was forced to meet his eyes. "Do you still dislike me?"

She hesitated and then decided to be honest. "Yes, I do. If

84

I weren't your wife, I'm sure Christopher wouldn't marry Maureen next week."

"You can't honestly believe that?"

"I do. If I were free now he wouldn't let you blackmail him!"

It was as though a shutter came down over Daniel's face. His hand dropped to his side and he returned to the armchair and picked up a journal.

"Close the door on your way out," he said quietly. "I'm going to read."

Resenting the curt dismissal, despite the fact that she had asked for it, Briony did as she was told.

Upstairs in her room she undressed and climbed into bed, feeling unusually small beneath the down-filled duvet. Did she believe what she had said to Daniel downstairs? Would Christopher have broken with Maureen if she herself were still single? Since their bitter discussion in the library on the first day of her marriage, they had never talked alone together, and neither by word nor gesture had he given her any indication that he still loved her. Yet how would she react if he tried to hold her in his arms the way he had done when she had believed him free to marry her? It was impossible to guess what she would feel, for in these four weeks she had come to regard him more and more as Daniel's brother and less and less as the man she had loved.

*Had* loved?

Why had she put the words in the past tense? What had happened to her? Trembling, she sat up in bed. Could she, like Fay, be developing a different character now that she was living in this elegant home, treated as its mistress even though she was not the wife of its master?

A picture of Daniel came so vividly to mind that he seemed to be in the room with her. Yet he had never even set foot in it. She clutched the eiderdown around her. Close to Daniel or not, he had such a strong personality that she had inevitably compared him with his brother – and found the brother wanting!

At last she was seeing Christopher for what he was: a good-looking man who allowed his brother to dictate to him. If she had had the opportunity of getting to know him better, she would have found this out much sooner. But they had parted while she was still blinded by his charm, and because of this, her love for him – a blind, obstinate love – had lingered on. But not any more. At last she was free. She belonged to no one except herself.

The relief was so great that all tension left her and she sank back on the pillow. Had she really stopped loving Christopher, or had the knowledge of his impending marriage made her close her mind to her need of him?

Deliberately she thought of him: his tall body and tanned skin; his blond hair and his mouth which had so frequently kissed her own. There was no stirring of her pulses; only a faint revulsion against herself for having been so blind to his intrinsic weakness. Content with the knowledge that she was genuinely heart-whole, she closed her eyes.

She was on the verge of sleep when she thought of Daniel again, and remembered that he had put a thousand pounds into her account. It was an inordinately extravagant amount to spend on a dress and fur, and she determined to tell him so in the morning. Only a few months ago she would have considered half that sum a fortune. She sat up sharply. What a fool she was! Here she was thinking about clothes when all the time the money – or certainly five hundred of it – could be used to clear Fay's debt to Mr. Van der Heim. Pleasure flooded through her. How delighted Fay would be! It was too late to go upstairs and tell her now, but she would do so first thing in the morning.

Steps sounded in the next room and she heard the click of a light switch. For all his intention of reading, Daniel had not stayed long in the library. She listened to him undressing, following his movements as doors and wardrobe were opened and closed. With what precision he emptied his pockets and prepared his things for the following morning. Even with a valet to look after him he did a great deal for himself. He's a perfectionist, she thought irritably, and doesn't think anyone can do anything as well as he can. There was a faint creak of springs, the light clicked again and there was silence.

Annoyance that Daniel should go to bed so calmly while she herself was still lying wakeful brought home to her the calibre of the man she had married. How little she knew of him! It was a frightening realisation and it filled her mind for a long while, making her wonder what the future held for them, and how long they would share it together.

# CHAPTER SEVEN

BRIONY had no chance to speak to Fay next morning, for she had such an early class that it was barely six-thirty when she crept downstairs. She was halfway across the hall when there was a step behind her, and she turned to see Marriot. "I hope you are not going to leave without breakfast?"

"I'll get some coffee at the theatre."

The chauffeur hesitated and then said: "Mr. Clayton is in the breakfast room."

Already at the front door, Briony stopped. To leave without going in to see Daniel would cause the sort of comment he wished to avoid.

"I hadn't realised he was already up."

"He's operating this morning, madam."

She nodded and went down the hall to the breakfast room. The December morning was still dark and the lights were on, casting a mellow glow over flowery chintz and patterned breakfast china. Daniel was at the table, a cup halfway to his lips, and he set it down in surprise as she came in.

"I'm off to early class," she explained.

"I'm glad to see you've left time for breakfast." Without waiting for her answer he went over to the sideboard and returned with a plate of grilled bacon, sausage and kidney.

"I couldn't eat all this!" she protested.

"You can't rehearse all morning on an empty stomach. Eat up."

He looked so fierce that she obeyed him, and after swallowing a mouthful realised with surprise that she was hungry. Quickly she cleared her plate, and only then did she speak.

"Do you always get up so early when you operate?"

"Yes. My first one's scheduled for eight." He glanced at his watch and stood up. In his dark suit and tie he reminded her of the man she had first met, for though the anger was no longer there, he still had an air of tension.

"Can I give you a lift?" he asked. "When Marriot has dropped me at Luther's he can take you on to the theatre."

"That would be marvellous."

Sitting beside him in his gleaming Rolls, she could not resist a smile as she wondered what the other members of the company would think if they could see her now – talk about the Prince and the Showgirl!

"What's amusing you?"

Unaware that Daniel had been looking at her, she coloured furiously, and without pressing the point he lapsed into silence, not speaking again until they swept through the hospital gates and he jumped from the car.

"Have a good day, Briony, and don't work too hard."

"Nor you," she murmured, and feeling distinctly regal, waved goodbye as they bowled out through the gates again en route for the theatre.

Surprisingly her marriage had caused little comment in the company, and she wondered if this was because no one had yet seen her husband. Although he was regarded as a king at the Luther Hospital and in the medical world, he was unimportant to the blinkered world of ballet. As an orthopaedic surgeon he would have commanded considerably more attention, for ballet dancers, like racehorses, were concerned with their limbs and if anyone discovered a good orthopaedic or manipulative surgeon, the name went round the company like wildfire.

"Is my husband always so tense when he operates?" she asked the chauffeur.

"It depends, madam. This morning he's operating on a youngster, and that always disturbs him."

"I didn't know he looked after children."

"This is a sixteen-year-old lad. A hopeless case, Mr .Clayton says."

"Then why is he operating?"

"There's always the chance of a miracle." The man was obviously quoting his employer. "Mr. Clayton doesn't feel he has the right to refuse."

Briony found it disturbing to visualise Daniel facing five or six hours of the utmost concentration, knowing he would certainly fail in the end. No wonder he had been so tense this morning. It amazed her that he could lay aside the burden of his responsibilities and play the role of host each night, for playing a role he certainly was! Since her marriage she had come to realise this very strongly, for watching him when he was unaware of it she had occasionally caught the weariness on his face and seen the bone tiredness of the man seeping through. It was ridiculous of him to insist on a formal dinner each evening. When he came home from the hospital – particularly after a day spent operating – he should have a quiet meal alone and not have to listen to chatter and gossip which he must find unutterably boring.

"I'll tell him so," she decided, and knew at once that she would do no such thing. He had not married her to be his wife in the true sense of the word, but to fulfil a part which he had designated for her: hostess and helpmate who would enable him to achieve the neurological wing he had set his heart on; not a woman to worry about his well-being.

She was glad when the car reached the theatre, and thanking Marriot, she hurried to the dressing-room to change into her practice clothes.

As usual the day was a continuous grind of work. A large part of the new ballet which Beloff was choreographing required considerable technical skill, for his determination to link modern steps with classical ones put a great strain on all the dancers.

Again and again Briony and her partner, Neil Halper, were

90

forced to repeat their steps, and they were both soaked with perspiration when they broke off for lunch.

"I won't need either of you this afternoon," Beloff said. "Go home and rest."

It was unexpected freedom and Briony decided to take advantage of it. She would pay Mr. Van der Heim the rest of the money Fay owed him, and then buy a dress and fur for Christopher's wedding.

Christopher's wedding. Incredible that she could think of it without any emotion except the relief of knowing it would take him away from the house.

It was soon after the lunch hour when she reached the jeweller's office, and climbing to the top of the old building she entered his workroom.

At sight of her he bounded forward, his round face beaming.

"I was delighted to get your phone call, Miss Stevens. I do not wish to make trouble for your sister, you understand, but the insurance company held me responsible for the loss of the necklace and —"

"Here's the cheque," Briony interrupted, and passed it over to him.

He looked at it, his mouth pursing as he saw she had signed the surname Clayton.

"I'm married," she explained.

"You have a generous husband."

She reddened but made no reply, anxious only to escape.

Not until she was in the street again, breathing deeply of the cold December air, did her tension ebb. Yet it had nothing to do with the jeweller. He had had to pay for the necklace himself, and the five hundred pounds was now rightfully his.

But it had not been rightfully hers to give: this was why she despised herself for what she had done. The money was Daniel's, given to her for a specific purpose, and she had misused it. Attacked by conscience, she hailed a taxi and drove

91

immediately to Bond Street, anxious to buy the smartest outfit she could find. But window-shopping along both sides of the street, she was appalled by the high prices, and decided it would be safer to buy her fur jacket first. Only when she had done so would she know what money she had left to spend on a dress.

Several hours later Briony regretfully knew she would never find the mink jacket Daniel had specified with the money left at her disposal. The amount given to Mr. Van der Heim had taken far too big a chunk. She had enough to buy a dress and accessories, but not enough to buy a mink.

"Why not consider another type of fur?" the furrier to whom she took her problem suggested. "These days it doesn't need to be mink to be smart."

To prove his point he darted across the salon and returned with a beautifully cut jacket the exact colour of her hair.

"It's beautiful," she said. "What fur is it?"

"Persian paw. They do them now in all colours. I have a dark blue one trimmed with silver buttons and –"

"This one's fine," Briony said hastily. "I'll take it."

With the jacket paid for, she was left with sufficient money to find the dress she wanted: a creamy beige wool with soft neckline and slender skirt. Beige shoes and bag and small hat in brown completed her outfit, and she then searched for something for Fay, finally choosing a scarlet wool two-piece.

"I've never worn such a bright colour before," Fay exclaimed doubtfully when she saw it. "It's gorgeous, but . . ."

"It's exactly right for you," Briony said firmly. "You're far too young to go on wearing dowdy colours."

"Cripples should be heard and not seen!"

"I've heard *you* too much!" Briony spoke with sisterly candour. "Now take the suit and stop arguing."

Fay held it against her, turning her body from side to side as she looked in the mirror. "You're right. It *does* things for me. You're so good to me, Briony. I never thought you'd buy me another new dress so soon."

"It's a celebration gift –"

"For Christopher's wedding," Fay interrupted with a giggle. "We really *are* lucky he let you down. If he hadn't, you wouldn't have met Daniel – and he's a hundred times nicer!"

Briony ignored the comment. "I was referring to something quite different when I said celebration. I've paid Mr. Van der Heim. We don't owe him another penny!"

Joy robbed Fay of speech, but her face glowed as though a lamp had been lit behind it. "Where – where did you get it from?" she stammered. "Was it Beloff?"

"It was from Daniel."

"You mean he knows about the necklace?" The glow disappeared from Fay's face. "Oh, Briony, I wish you hadn't told him. Now he'll know I was the one who blackmailed Chris."

"He doesn't know anything." Briony caught her sister's shoulder and gave it a reassuring squeeze, feeling ten years older than her instead of two years younger. "Daniel knows nothing about your call to Christopher. He still thinks it was me. But he gave me some money to buy myself a mink jacket and dress for the wedding and I decided to use some of it to pay off the necklace."

"He'll be furious when he finds out."

"He won't know. He never asks me how I spend my allowance."

"But a thousand pounds!" Fay was still unconvinced. "He'll want to see *something* for that amount."

"I bought a dress and a lovely fur jacket," Briony assured her. "I promise you he'll be delighted with it." She paused and then decided to say something that had been in her mind for several weeks. "I don't know why you worry if Daniel found out it was *you* who telephoned Christopher. If we explained that you had wanted the money to pay for the necklace –"

"No!" It was an emphatic sound. "He thinks it was you.

You told him you wanted the money to get us a better flat. There's no reason for us to change the story."

"But the truth —"

"How do you know he'd believe us?"

"He could ask Mr. Van der Heim," Briony said.

"And find out what a stupid fool I was? I don't want him to know. You promised me you wouldn't tell him! You promised!" Fay was hysterical now, her body shaking as much as her voice. "Daniel's the only person who thinks I'm normal. He treats me like an adult — a woman instead of a child. If he finds out I lost the necklace — that I called Christopher and then let *you* take the blame. . . ." Sobs drowned her words and she rocked backwards and forwards with misery. "I don't want him to know what I did . . . he'll despise me."

Briony realised it was a waste of time to try and make Fay see she was wrong. When her sister was in this mood, logic had no bearing on reality.

"There's no need to cry," she said firmly. "If you feel so strongly about it we won't say a word to him. It doesn't matter to me what Daniel thinks."

Happy again, Fay's tears dried. "He still married you — so he can't think all that badly of you!" The peaky face grew curious. "Are things still the same between you?"

"Why should they change?"

"All things change with time," came the answer, "and I also think you've stopped caring for Christopher."

"You're right about *that*!"

"Then what about you and Daniel? Do you think you could —"

"No!" Briony said sharply, and walked to the door. "I'm going to have a rest. Shopping is more tiring than dancing."

Alone in her room she was uneasily aware how close Daniel was to her each night; a soft call and he could hear her, a few steps and he could be at her side. Curiously she wondered why he had never married before, and remembered his reply when she had asked him why he had chosen *her* instead of someone from a well-known and well-endowed family: with his looks and reputation he would not have had any problem about choice.

"A woman who has a great deal to offer," he had answered, "wants a great deal in return. And I have nothing to give. My life is devoted to my work."

During the first few weeks of their marriage she had believed him, but since getting to know him she was convinced there was another reason behind his refusal to commit himself to one person.

Restlessly she got off the bed and went down to the drawing-room in search of a magazine. To her surprise Mrs. Clayton – who normally spent the hours before dinner in her own room – was lying on a settee sewing at a small piece of gros-point.

"How nice to see you, Briony," she welcomed. "Have you come to keep me company?"

Sensing loneliness in the words, Briony nodded and sat down. "I had the afternoon off and went shopping," she said. "I bought a dress for the wedding."

"I wish I'd been able to go to Daniel's wedding. I looked forward to it for so long."

"I'm sure he didn't realise you'd be so upset at missing it," Briony said awkwardly.

"Daniel realises everything. He's the most sensitive man I know. Surely *you* know that!"

"Not really," Briony said cautiously.

"You will once you've gained more confidence with him. At the moment you still can't understand why he married you."

"I never will."

"One reason is because you're so different from –" The thin voice stopped, but Briony was determined to hear the end of the sentence.

"Because I'm different from whom? Was Daniel engaged before?" She forced herself to smile. "I'm not jealous of his past, you know. After all, I was the one he married!"

Uncertainty still masked Mrs. Clayton's features, but after a moment she set down her needlework and spoke. "Daniel fell in love when he was thirty. She was the daughter of one of our friends and a very beautiful girl. It would have been an ideal marriage except that she wanted him to set up in Harley Street. But he had other ideas. There was a professor in Canada whose methods he wanted to study, and it meant living for a couple of years in some prairie town miles from anywhere."

"Sounds an unlikely place for an eminent professor," Briony could not help remarking.

"We thought so too, but apparently it was a special clinic and fantastically well equipped."

"A place after Daniel's own heart." Briony did not realise how dry her voice sounded until she saw Mrs. Clayton look at her, and she coloured and said: "I mean, he – he's now trying to get the same sort of place for himself." She paused and then asked: "Wouldn't the girl go with him?"

"No. She insisted he either gave up the idea completely or she'd give *him* up. The next we knew was that Daniel took himself off to Canada for two years. When he came back he was like he is now: extremely ambitious and withdrawn." The grey-blonde head tilted to one side. "But you've made a great difference to him, Briony. Even in a few short weeks he's more relaxed – especially when you're at home. The nights you dance at the theatre and he's too busy to see you, he gets very tetchy."

"Why doesn't he tell me when he's coming to the theatre?" Briony burst out.

"Perhaps he's still afraid to let you know how much he cares for you."

It was a logical remark for Mrs. Clayton to make, believing as she did that her stepson's marriage was a normal one. But to Briony it made no sense. The knowledge that Daniel came to watch her every time she danced a solo role had nagged at her mind since she had learned of it.

"He takes great delight in your progress," the older woman went on. "He's going to give you a big party the night you dance the première of Mr. Beloff's new ballet."

Briony's breath came out on a sigh. At last she knew the reason for Daniel's interest in her career. As a ballerina she would be the jewel in his crown, drawing admiring glances which would in turn lead to monetary donations that would help him achieve his ambition. So abruptly that she sent the chair rocking, she stood up, and bright brown eyes looked at her in alarm.

"You're not upset because I told you Daniel was once engaged? It was years ago. It doesn't mean a thing to him now."

"It isn't that," Briony said hurriedly. "But I just remembered I have to make a phone call."

She returned to her bedroom, but her anger against Daniel had disappeared as quickly as it had come, and she found herself thinking of his broken romance. She was certain he had not forgotten this unknown girl. If he had, he would not be so determined to keep emotion out of his life.

She must have fallen into a doze, for she awoke to hear sounds from Daniel's bedroom and knew he had come home from the hospital and was changing for dinner. In this day and age it had seemed an anachronism to put on a dinner jacket each evening, but his terse reply to her comment on it had made her feel childish.

"When you've been operating and visiting sick people all day you like to get the smell of the hospital out of your bones. And if I'm going to bathe and change it might as well be into a dinner jacket."

"I hadn't seen it like that," she had apologised.

"You don't see a lot of things, Briony."

His answer had puzzled her, and for several days afterwards she had pondered on its meaning, finally dismissing it as one more of his enigmatic remarks.

Now as she heard the sound of bath water she decided to go downstairs ahead of him; anything to avoid leaving her room at the same time as he did. Putting on a long cream woollen skirt and pure silk shirt blouse in the same colour, she ran down to the drawing-room, stopping in dismay as she saw that Christopher was alone.

"Where's your mother?"

"She was tired and Daniel said she should have dinner in bed. And Maureen is dining alone with her dear papa, which means you and Daniel will have me all to yourselves." His eyes glinted. "But at the moment you can have me strictly to *yourself.*"

"Don't bother flirting with me." She moved across to the fireplace, her head barely reaching the lintel. She was aware of him watching her, and returned his gaze without her usual tremor.

"You've changed a lot since you married Daniel," he said abruptly.

"Marriage must be good for me."

"How did you know I meant it for the better?"

"I'm sure you didn't mean anything else!"

He shrugged. "You're right, as a matter of fact. You've developed more spirit and it suits you."

"It's a pity I didn't have more spirit when I first met you. You mightn't have played such havoc with my life."

"Briony darling, I was —"

"Don't pretend you ever loved me," she interrupted.

"But I did — I do."

"The way you love cream cakes or chocolate! You don't love me — not the real me."

"You're talking nonsense," he said sulkily. "We'd have been happy together if things had been different. We got on well."

"Because we never had any reason to quarrel. But I don't

98

think we'd have been happy. We're too different." She paused, head on one side as she looked at him. "I can't see you sitting alone night after night while I dance at the theatre."

"You can say that again! If we'd got married you'd have had to give it up."

She was amazed by his conceit. Did he honestly believe he could have ordered her to give up her dancing? Words failed her. Not that words were necessary any longer. Her love for Christopher was like a dream; it had given her pleasure and pain while it lasted, but now she was awake and knew it had never been reality.

"I guess you're more suited to Daniel than I realised." Christopher was standing by the sideboard pouring a drink, and he brought it over and handed it to her. "You're both a couple of untouchables." He touched her cheek lightly. "Don't let yourself be consumed by ambition the way my dear brother is. Deep down you're a warm, emotional girl. That much I do remember." His eyes stared into hers. "What's happened to that warmth? Will you find someone else to give it to, or will you go on with this pretence of a marriage?"

A sound at the door made them turn. Daniel stood on the threshold, his pale face impassive. With easy nonchalance Christopher took his hand from her cheek, but Briony still felt as though his finger was burning on it, and she lowered her eyes and sipped her drink.

"Whisky for you, Daniel?" Christopher asked easily.

"Please. A double."

At this Briony looked up. Daniel was abstemious, contenting himself with a light aperitif and a couple of glasses of wine at dinner. For him to drink a large whisky was unusual, particularly on a day when he had been operating and might be called out if an emergency arose. Looking at him as he crossed to the other side of the fireplace she was aware that his pallor had a grey tinge, as it always did when he was tired or upset. An unexpected surge of anxiety for him overcame her embarrassment that he had witnessed her scene with Christopher.

"How did the operation go?" she asked.

"I did three," he said impassively.

"Well, how did they all go?"

"Two were successful. One wasn't. "

"Was that the one on the young boy? Marriot told me about it."

"Marriot's developed a morbid curiosity in my patients," Daniel said with a slight smile.

"Only in the ones you're concerned about."

"I'm concerned for them all."

Knowing he was being deliberately obtuse she said firmly: "There are some you worry about more than others. You don't regard your patients as if they're numbers!"

"I try to keep my feelings apart from my work. It's the only way to make sure your judgement isn't clouded. Feelings are a part of *your* professional life, Briony, not mine."

"Daniel's right," Christopher said, refilling his own glass and coming to stand beside them. "Think how awful it would be if you started cutting someone up and remembered that you couldn't stand his politics – or were crazy about his wife!"

Briony could not help smiling, but there was no amusement on Daniel's face, and she knew without being told that the young boy whose case he had considered hopeless was hopeless indeed. Deciding not to belabour a subject he obviously did not want to talk about, she did not refer to it again, even when they were left alone while Christopher went to take a call from Maureen.

"I'm sorry I came in at an inopportune moment," Daniel said. "You and Christopher were obviously enjoying your tête-à-tête."

"It wasn't what you thought."

"I thought you were getting over him," Daniel said harshly, "but it seems you haven't. You're still a fool!"

100

His biting sarcasm decided her against telling him the truth. "I'd rather have too much emotion than none at all. At least as a person I'm alive."

"Meaning?"

"That you're a cold fish with water in your veins!"

He laughed; an unpleasant sound that made her angrier. "You've cocooned yourself from the world, Daniel. Because you had one unhappy love affair, you think –"

"Leave my love life out of it."

"Why should I? If you can discuss mine, I can discuss yours!" She was riding high on temper. "You're a fine one to talk about *me* not getting over a love affair. You were jilted years ago, yet you're still scared to death of getting involved with anyone else."

"Be quiet!" With surprising speed Daniel lunged forward, but as his hands came out to grip her, Christopher came back into the room, grinning as he saw their flushed faces.

"Have I interrupted a lovers' quarrel?"

"Oh, be quiet!" Briony cried.

"Yes, ma'am. Actually I came in to say I won't be in to dinner after all. I'm going over to Maureen."

He sauntered out, and immediately Briony moved over to the door. "I'm going to my room. Perhaps you'll ask the butler to let me know when Tom arrives."

"He isn't coming," Daniel said. "I was going to tell you when I came in, but. . . . The doctor who usually stands in for him is ill."

"I see." She hesitated. "I'm sorry. I know you wanted to talk to him about Fay."

"I already have. I took his call and used the opportunity to have a word with him. He's promised to let me have Fay's case history. I suggested he came to dinner during the week and brought it with him."

"It's kind of you to bother." She opened the door. "As there'll only be the two of us in the dining room tonight, I'll have my dinner on a tray. It's been a long day and I'm going to bed."

Not waiting for his agreement, she closed the door with a snap and ran up the stairs.

# CHAPTER EIGHT

CHRISTOPHER'S wedding day dawned bright and clear with a pale lemon sun shining in a pale blue sky. The ceremony was at St. George's, Hanover Square, and the reception at Sir Geoffrey Hirst's home in Mayfair.

The ceremony was scheduled for noon and Briony was still dressing when Daniel and Christopher left for the church. Tom Bristow was calling to collect her and Fay and Mrs. Clayton, though she was the only one ready to greet him when he arrived.

It was the first time she had seen him since he had dined at the house last week-end, and he talked about Daniel immediately.

"I always knew he was a brilliant surgeon, but I wasn't sure how I'd react to him being your husband."

She looked at him speculatively, wondering if Fay had told him what sort of marriage it was. But there was nothing to suggest this from his expression, which was frank and guileless.

"Living here has made a great difference to Fay," she said quickly.

He nodded. "I'd hardly take her for the same girl."

As though his words had conjured her up, Fay came into the room, looking unusually vibrant in her new red suit. In the last few weeks her face had filled out and her hair had lost its drabness. Cut short, it swung against her cheeks each time she moved her head. Only as she limped forward did Briony realise with a pang that certain things hadn't changed.

"Robin redbreast herself," Tom grinned. "I've never seen you look so perky."

"Do you like it?"

Though lameness prevented her from twirling in front of him, Fay moved so that her skirt swung provocatively around her legs: beautiful legs, slim and supple so long as she remained still.

"Who can help liking it?" he replied. "You don't look a day over eighteen."

"I'll be twenty-five next month," Fay sniffed. "I'm already an old maid. Not that I'll mind if Briony gives me lots of nephews and nieces."

Briony's warmth towards her sister cooled, but she said nothing until Tom had gone downstairs to switch on the heater in his car. Only then did she show her irritation.

"It's been bad enough having Christopher make suggestive remarks about me and Daniel, but for you to do the same! For heaven's sake, Fay, you know very well my marriage isn't real."

"More fool you. Daniel's longing to be loved."

"So am I," Briony said tartly, "but we don't long to be loved by each other!"

"Are you sure?"

"What's that supposed to mean?"

"Merely that you light up like a torch when Daniel's in the room."

"If you mean I act as if I'm aware of him," Briony said evenly, "then I agree. But it isn't because I love him: it's because he's watching me all the time – making sure I don't let him down."

"I wish he'd watch me the way he watches you!"

"And I wish you'd stop day-dreaming."

"I just want you to be happy," Fay said. "You don't love Christopher and I thought Daniel could take his place."

"Just like that, eh? Off with the old and on with the new?"

"Why not? I know you'll tell me off for interfering, but –" Fay looked unexpectedly serious. "Sometimes I think I was to blame for your falling for Christopher. I saw him as the answer to my dreams and what I felt rubbed off on you — made you invest him with a strength he doesn't have. Not the way Daniel has."

"Please stop talking about Daniel," Briony said as quietly as she could. "My marriage is a business arrangement. Nothing more." Giving Fay no chance to answer, she went out to the car.

Maureen's wedding was a splendid affair with no expense spared, and remembering her own bleak wedding and unsmiling bridegroom, Briony knew a pang of self-pity. Refusing to give way to it, she focussed her eyes on Daniel's back. How commanding he looked next to Christopher, and how much more confident a woman would feel to have him as a husband. Yet he *was* her husband, she reminded herself, though he did not require her to be a proper wife. Unwillingly she wondered how he would act if he fell in love again. Could passion warm those cool and appraising eyes and bring the colour to his pale skin? Resolutely she brought her mind back to the service and the people around her. How beautifully dressed the women were; most of them in full-length furs with here and there a brocade or silk. Briony's satisfaction with her own appearance began to fade and the fur jacket that had looked so lovely when seen in her own mirror now looked the cheap little fur it was. A "fun fur" the furrier had called it, and foolishly she had been delighted by the name, forgetting that this was not what Daniel had meant her to buy. Not that she didn't look well-groomed and pretty, she assured herself, but she lacked the gloss she knew was expected from the wife of an eminent surgeon.

In a gathering like this, one must be either fashionable or extremely unfashionable; both were acceptable. To look as if one were trying and failing was the final sin.

During the reception Briony was introduced to so many people that she had no time to think of her appearance. Here was a golden opportunity for Daniel to show her off as his

105

wife, and he took advantage of it, moving with her from group to group.

Sir Geoffrey came over to speak to her a second time when he saw she was momentarily left alone – Daniel having been commandeered by a dowager in sable and diamonds. He spent several moments extolling Daniel's virtues and then abruptly switched to the subject of the new neurological wing.

"Your husband won't rest until he's got it. He's extremely single-minded!"

"What are his chances?" Briony asked politely, marvelling that she was able to disguise her abhorrence of Daniel's obsession.

"Very good. Luther's can afford to build the wing and install some of the equipment provided Daniel can raise the other half million that's needed. He doesn't only want a sterile operating theatre, you know. He's determined to have sterile post-operative care too. Highly commendable, of course, but where does one get the money?" He gave a bark of laughter. "He'll succeed, though, I've no doubt of it."

Briony had no doubt either; particularly when Daniel – extracting her from Sir Geoffrey – led her towards a swarthy, middle-aged couple who he informed her were George Leonadis the Greek shipping magnate, and his sister.

"I'm relying on you to charm them," he whispered.

"Is *he* going to be your provider?"

"I hope so." Daniel's eyes were glittering with a brightness she had never seen before, though she was not sure if it was caused by excitement or anger. They were now abreast of the couple and he made the introductions and then concentrated on the woman, leaving Briony to talk to the man.

The Greek was witty and had an excellent command of English. Shrewdness marked his heavy features and his small black eyes appraised her.

"We have seen you dance," he said. "My sister recognised

you. You took over when Davina was ill with food poisoning, didn't you?"

"How did you know?"

"We are balletomanes like your husband. That is how I met Daniel. We were both guests of Lord Hackleton." The way he stressed the title told Briony that this bull-like, aggressive man had a chink in his armour, and as he continued talking, peppering the conversation with more titles, she saw why Daniel had such high hopes that Leonadis would donate the money he needed. The Greek was a naturalised British subject and hoped to buy himself into the Honours List.

"You and Daniel must come and spend a weekend with us," Leonadis was saying. "I have just bought Knowlebarn."

Briony looked blank, but Daniel came swiftly to her rescue.

"You were lucky to buy such a wonderful old house, George. When families can't afford to keep up estates like that they usually pass them over to the National Trust."

"Cavenham needed the money," Chryssoula Leonadis said, waving a ringed hand in the air. "He's taken his half million and emigrated to Australia."

"So now we all have what we want," her brother concluded. "Cavenham his money, and I the home I have wanted all my life."

"Don't you miss Greece?" Briony asked.

"No. I love England and your Royal Family."

Briony knew he meant every word, and she found it odd yet charming. Expecting to dislike him for his snobbishness, she found him so obvious about it that it was amusing. He certainly enjoyed his money, and helped other people to enjoy it too, for he was telling them now of the orphanage he had built and his insistence that each child be bought a suit or dress each winter and summer.

"I wore rags until I was fifteen," he said, patting his barrel chest. "And when my shirt had to be washed I couldn't go out till it was dry!"

"Those were the old days," his sister said, anxious to change the subject. "Forget the past."

"The past has made me what I am today and put us both here – able to talk to this beautiful dancer and our great friend Daniel." He turned to Briony. "He is the best neuro-surgeon in the world. But then I'm sure you know that!"

A tinge of colour marked Daniel's cheeks and, noticing it, Briony wondered if it came from pleasure or embarrassment. Embarrassment, she learned, as he led her across the room to meet someone else, for he gave an apologetic laugh and said:

"George will insist on talking about me as if I'm the only neuro-surgeon in the world."

"He obviously has a reason for thinking you're so good." His only answer was a shrug, and new people and more conversation prevented her from asking him anything more.

By five o'clock Briony was so exhausted that she wondered nervously if she would be able to dance tonight. And she was the Sugar Plum Fairy!

"What's wrong?" Daniel asked. "You're rubbing your leg."

"I'm tired," she said hesitantly.

"And you're dancing tonight, aren't you?" At her nod, he frowned. "Forgive me, Briony. I'm a fool for not realising it. But Christopher and Maureen are leaving in a moment and we can go straight home afterwards." There was an odd expression in his eyes. "Unless you'd like to leave before they do?"

Misunderstanding him, she shook her head. "I'll wait."

Only as she uttered the words did she guess that he had been asking her if she could bear to see Christopher and Maureen leave for their honeymoon. Would he believe her if she told him she was delighted, or would he think that pride was forcing her to pretend she no longer loved his brother?

But there was no pretence about her pleasure as she waved them goodbye, nor in her loud wishes for their happiness.

Standing beside her, Fay gave a sigh. "It was a beautiful

wedding. I wish I could have one like it."

"Choose the right man and you will," Tom answered. He was talking to Daniel but had evidently not missed the remark.

"Who'd want *me*?" Fay retorted.

"Lots of men," Tom grinned, and put up his hand to tweak her hair before he realised it was no longer hanging down her back. "You'd better keep a little bit hanging especially for me to pull," he teased. "I don't mind you changing into a beauty so long as there's still something about you I can recognise." His grin became more mischievous. "Though as your doctor I can probably recognise more than most!"

"That's a very unprofessional thing to say," Fay replied with all her old sharpness, and went to swing round. The movement caught her off balance and her leg gave way.

Tom's arm came out with lightning speed and steadied her. "You must learn not to lose your temper," he murmured. "I didn't mean to upset you. After all, I *am* your doctor."

"I don't need you to be. I've got Daniel!"

"He won't take your temperature and make you say ninety-nine the way I do," Tom said, still managing to retain his humour.

"Maybe he won't. But he doesn't treat me like a patient the whole time. He *does* remember I'm a person."

"So do I," Tom protested, "and a very pretty person too." He was still supporting her by the waist and he gave her a squeeze. "Come and have dinner with me tonight and I'll prove it."

"Don't be silly. Why should I have dinner with you?"

"Because *I'm* a person too." His sandy brows waggled up and down. "It's all very well you saying I treat you like a patient, but what about you always treating me like a doctor?"

"You're caught fair and square," Daniel chuckled. "You can't refuse his invitation now."

"Oh, very well," Fay said with a lack of grace she had not

109

displayed since the old days in the flat. "But you can't take me dancing the way you could Briony."

"I know your limitations better than you do, funny face. And if you don't sweeten your tongue a bit, we'll end up dining at the scorpions' table at the zoo!"

Against her will Fay laughed, and the sound of it was still in Briony's ears as she returned to Cumberland Terrace with Daniel and Mrs. Clayton.

"If I weren't living with you," Mrs. Clayton said to her stepson, "you and Briony could have a proper married life. I really feel I should move into a small flat."

"A penthouse in Mayfair, no doubt," Daniel said dryly.

"Well, I like to be somewhere central and I do like to sit in the sun," she murmured, "but I wouldn't look for a flat you couldn't afford."

"You can have two penthouses if you want," Daniel replied seriously. "The income from the engineering business is yours, Sylvie, even though you keep refusing to spend it."

"You're already too generous to me."

"You've been generous to me, Sylvie." Daniel caught hold of his stepmother's hand. "If you like, now that Christopher's gone we can turn the top floor into a self-contained flat for you."

"You'll be needing that as a nursery suite."

"When the time comes," he said without any show of embarrassment, "your present rooms can be divided into a day and night nursery."

"What do *you* think, Briony?" Mrs. Clayton asked.

"I agree with Daniel," Briony said stonily.

Composedly the woman shook her head. "I saw you chatting up George Leonadis," she said, unexpectedly changing the conversation. "I assume you're planning a dinner party for him?"

"Yes, I am. I'd like you to help Briony arrange it. A black tie affair and as many titles as possible."

"Won't that make Mr. Leonadis feel uncomfortable?" Briony asked, as the car drew to a stop outside the house.

"That's the whole idea!" Daniel escorted the two women into the hall. "George has given away at least a million without getting the title he wants and I'm hoping to persuade him that another half million to the Luther will do the trick!"

"I'm sure you'll succeed." Briony went towards the lift with Mrs. Clayton, but Daniel stopped her.

"I'd like to talk to you for a moment," he said, and opened the library door.

Silently she went inside. "I'm very tired, Daniel," she murmured, sitting down. "Can't it wait until I come home tonight?"

"I'd rather say it now." He raked her from head to toe. "Why didn't you buy a *mink* jacket?"

The unexpectedness of the question confounded her.

"I expressly asked you to buy one," he went on, "and you expressively disregarded my wishes."

"Why is it necessary to have mink?" she countered, beginning to gather her wits.

"As my wife, you're expected to —"

"Don't be so old-fashioned," she interrupted. "People can wear anything these days. It's far more fashionable *not* to wear fur than to wear it!"

"Maybe so. But if you *are* wearing fur, I'd like it to be something better than skunk!"

"It isn't skunk! It's Persian paw and it's very pretty."

"For a teenager, perhaps. Not for Mrs. Daniel Clayton."

Angrily she took off her jacket and faced him. "How about the dress? Or don't you like that either?"

"There's nothing wrong with it." His eyes moved from her face and slowly travelled the length of her body. "With your figure you'd look beautiful in a sack."

The compliment was so unexpected that her heart gave a thump.

111

"But that's beside the point," he continued. "If you don't think you're the type for mink and you'd prefer to dress more simply, then by all means do so. But for heaven's sake don't try and mimic expensive fashion by wearing cheap copies!"

She caught her breath. "I'll dress the way you want me to, Daniel. I assume it was part of our bargain."

The ringing of the telephone cut across his answer and he picked it up, signalling for her to remain.

She did so, and saw his face grow thunderous as he talked, though when he finally replaced the receiver he did it with his usual quiet manner.

"So it wasn't prejudice that prevented you from buying mink," he said. "You obviously wished to spend the money on someone else." He took a step towards her. "Who is he?" he demanded. "Why did you give a man a cheque for five hundred pounds?"

Astonished, she stared at him. "How do you – who told you?"

"The manager of my bank. He just rang. Shortly before closing time a man came in with a cash cheque of yours for five hundred pounds. The cashier refused to pay it because you hadn't made it out properly and the manager rang to make sure it was really yours."

"Yes," she stammered, "it was."

"Who did you give the money too?"

Briony bit her lip. To tell Daniel it was Mr. Van der Heim would also mean telling him about the necklace Fay had lost. And once he learned this – and the value of the necklace – it wouldn't take him long to realise where Christopher's two and a half thousand pounds had gone. Nor would it take him long to guess it was Fay who had demanded it.

"Well?" Daniel repeated. "Who did you give the money to?"

Still she hesitated, remembering her promise to Fay. "It was a friend of mine."

112

"That much I gathered! You don't give five hundred to a stranger. All I want to know is *why* you gave it to him."

"I'd – I'd rather not answer you."

"Are you being blackmailed?"

"Of course not!" She was aghast at his misconception of the truth, but could think of no way of disabusing him.

"If you're in trouble," Daniel continued more quietly, "you must let me help you. I'm your husband and –"

"I don't need your help. Why can't you forget it?" she pleaded. "It's over and done with!"

"Then why keep it a secret? What are you afraid of?"

"I'm *not* afraid. In future I'll let you have bills for every single penny I spend!"

"I'm not concerned with what you spend in the future! It's what you've *just* spent I want to know about! Out with it, Briony. You're not leaving here till you've told me the truth." He came towards her menacingly, his expression so furious that she backed away from him.

"If you touch me I'll scream!" she gasped.

"*Who was it?*" he grated, and caught her shoulders in an iron grip. "Was it hush-money to an ex-boy-friend?"

"You're crazy!"

"Am I? Is it so crazy to assume you've had other men apart from Christopher?"

Apart from Christopher. The words resounded in her head like a clanging bell, and she looked at Daniel in horror. So he believed Christopher had been her lover! How naïve of her not to have realised this before. Remembering the way Christopher had referred to her when questioned by his mother she should have guessed that this interpretation would be put on their relationship. But somehow she had expected Daniel to form his *own* assessment of her. They had lived in the same house for two months; had shared many thoughts and moods. But none of it had affected his opinion of her character: he was as blind about her as he had always been.

"Well," he said, "I'm waiting for you to answer me."

"Believe what you want to believe," she replied and, pushing past him, ran from the room.

Upstairs she flung herself on the bed and lay there weeping, overcome by a desolation she could not understand. Only the knowledge that she had to go to the theatre gave her the strength to change and leave the house, creeping away from it like a thief in the night.

But once in the crowded dressing-room everything was forgotten, and she applied make-up and put on her costume with calm fingers. Nothing mattered to her except her dancing. She had determined on this when Christopher had let her down, and it was madness to let herself be destroyed all over again by another man. Especially one who meant nothing to her at all!

At the end of the performance the usual hired car – which Daniel had insisted she always take – was waiting to drive her home, and she sat slumped in the corner of it, her depression returning now that the excitement of the ballet was over. Only as the car swung into Cumberland Terrace did she notice a chink of light coming through the drawn curtains of the library window, and knowing that Daniel must still be up, she ordered the car to stop at once, and went quietly on foot for the rest of the way. The last thing in the world she wanted was for Daniel to hear her come in. If he continued the row to-night she would have hysterics and say things she might regret; things that would make it impossible for her and Fay to remain here. Carefully inserting her key in the lock, she entered the hall and went towards the stairs.

Her hand was on the banister when a long thin one covered it. Without raising her head she knew to whom it belonged.

"I've been waiting for you," Daniel said, and pulled her gently into the library. For a moment he stood looking at her, irritation and tenderness playing across his features.

"I'm not in the mood for another argument, Daniel." Was

114

this her voice speaking? Briony wondered. This thin, quivering whisper. She cleared her throat and said loudly: "If you intend continuing it, could you possibly wait until the morning?"

"No. What I have to say must be said now. Sit down."

Nervously she rubbed her hand across her forehead and walked across to a chair. It seemed an enormous distance away and she swayed and caught at the edge of the table. Instantly she felt herself being lifted and carried the remaining few yards.

"You'll feel better when you've had something to eat," he said in the same quiet tone he had used ever since she had come in. "I suppose you didn't eat anything before you went to the theatre?"

She did not answer and lay with closed eyes, listening to a gurgling sound of liquid and the clatter of a plate.

"Sit up and get this inside you."

Opening her eyes, she saw he had placed a small table in front of her. On it was a tray with a silver thermos flask, a thick slice of foie gras on a mound of golden aspic and several croissants wrapped in a warm napkin.

"Fattening the calf before the kill," she commented before she could stop herself.

His eyes gleamed and, in the light of a nearby standard lamp, looked more green than hazel. But he did not answer her, merely signalled her to eat and sat down on a chair opposite.

Afraid to disobey him, she pecked at a roll, but once she began she found she was hungry and had soon cleared the tray. Only when she had done so did he speak.

"If you hadn't been so confoundedly obstinate, Briony, you would have saved us both a lot of anguish."

"I don't understand you."

"I know you don't. That's always been the trouble." He looked rueful. "But I daresay I'm not an easy man to understand. I always believe I'm making myself perfectly clear, and yet...."

"You're not being clear now."

"I'm sorry, but what I have to say doesn't come easily. I owe you an apology." He leaned forward, his knees almost touching hers. "I should never have spoken to you the way I did earlier this evening."

"Forget it. It doesn't matter."

"It matters very much. You see, Fay came in to see me tonight after Tom brought her home."

Briony clutched eagerly at her sister's name. "I hope she had a good time. Where did Tom take her?"

"She'll give you those answers herself. It's the other things she said to me that are important."

"Other things?"

With an abruptness she had not seen in him before, he stood up and began to pace the room, not in the panther way he usually walked but like a tiger: swiftly, tensely, anger barely controlled.

"She came to tell me she's willing to go into hospital again. That she'll have any tests necessary to see if there's the faintest chance of her being able to walk normally."

"That's wonderful!" Briony forgot her own problems at hearing this news. "A few days ago I begged her to let me talk to you or Tom, but she wouldn't hear of it."

"Apparently she feels differently now."

"Was it Tom who persuaded her?"

"Tom had something to do with it, but it was mainly you." Daniel stopped pacing and focused his eyes on her. They were glittering and sharp like jewels. "Once she knew you'd completely paid for the necklace she felt able to cope with herself again. To quote her exactly, she said that your paying Van der Heim the last five hundred had taken a huge boulder off her shoulders."

Briony's heart began to beat fast and she stared down at the carpet. "So now you know I didn't give the money to my lover!"

"I know a lot more too. Fay told me *she* made that phone call to Christopher. She said she'd wanted to tell me weeks ago but couldn't pluck up the courage. Apparently knowing the necklace was completely paid for – and that you were responsible for it – made her feel she couldn't let you take the blame any more. I gather she told Tom about it tonight and then came back here to tell *me*."

"Poor Fay," Briony whispered, knowing what an effort it must have cost her sister to do so. Whenever Fay did things in a temper she either pretended she hadn't done them or begged Briony to take the blame for her. But tonight – for the first time – she had accepted responsibility for her own actions. It was heart-warming to know. Only one thing marred her pleasure, and she forced herself to raise her head and look at the broad-shouldered man in front of her. "Were you angry with her, Daniel?"

"I was so delighted I could have kissed her!"

"Delighted?"

"That call to Christopher was the one thing I couldn't associate with you," he went on. "After I got to know you – to understand you a little – I couldn't imagine you using threats to get money from him. Not even to help Fay! In the last few weeks I began to suspect the truth, but I wasn't sure."

"Why didn't you ask Christopher?"

"The last thing in the world I wanted was to talk to my brother about you!" His sigh was deep and audible. "I must have been crazy this evening when I accused you of having a lover. I hope you'll forgive me."

She nodded and, without knowing why, decided that as the air was being cleared it had better be cleared completely. With so many of Daniel's misconceptions gone to the wind she would dispose of the final one.

"Christopher was never my lover either. He wanted – he

117

tried, but . . . I'm still a virgin," she said clearly. "Perhaps not in physical terms because dancers often –" her cheeks were hot, but she looked at him with steadfast eyes. "You know what I mean."

"Yes," he said gravely, "I do. That's another apology I owe you."

"Perhaps you won't judge people so harshly in future."

"I try not to judge them at all. I've always prided myself on using logic unimpaired by feeling."

"You didn't do so with me," she retorted.

"*You* are not 'people'." He was standing close beside her, leaning down, his breath warm on the top of her hair. "In fact, my dear Briony, you're in a class of your own." His hand was heavy on her head, stroking the thick hair so that the few pins which confined it on the nape of her neck scattered to the ground and her hair swung around her in an amber-gold cloud.

"Such lovely hair," he said huskily, and touched his lips to it. It was the first gesture of affection he had displayed to her and she trembled. "And such a lovely innocent face," he went on, and tilted her chin to look into her eyes.

How could she have thought they were like Christopher's? she wondered. The colour was the same, but the expression was quite different. Here was not a man who lightly gave his affection but someone who – once he gave it – would be irrevocably committed: no wonder he held himself aloof, choosing to be lonely rather than risk being hurt again.

"Daniel, I –"

She could say no more, for he pulled her up into his arms and covered her mouth with his. For a moment she resisted, then as the pressure increased her lips relaxed and parted.

Feeling her response, he drew her closer, his fingers moving gently across her back and down her spine, caressing the curve of her thigh and moving up again to touch the soft fullness of her breasts.

Christopher had made love to her, but she had never felt it to be as intimate as it was with Daniel. There was no wild hunger here, no blind passion that could have been assuaged by any beautiful body. This desire was tempered by tenderness, by compassion for her tiredness after a long day.

Slowly Daniel drew back and, sitting in the chair she had vacated, pulled her on to his lap. Overcome by shyness, she stiffened, but he caught her close so that her head curved naturally against his neck.

"I haven't had a holiday for two years," he said. "What are your chances of getting time off?"

"To go on holiday with you?"

"I wasn't suggesting wc went separately!"

She looked up at him and knew she was being teased. Teased by Daniel. It was unbelievable yet strangely exciting.

"I'm not suggesting it's platonic either," he added, and this time there was no teasing in his eyes. "You're my wife, Briony, and I'd like to make our marriage a real one."

"But –"

"Don't give me your answer now," he said quickly. "I know it wasn't part of our bargain, but I've – I'm sure we can be happy together." Still holding her, he stood up and set her on her feet. "You're as high as my heart."

She sighed. "What a lovely thing to say!"

"I can think of other lovely things! But not tonight. You're sleeping on your feet and I'm wicked to keep you from your bed. Come, I'll put you into it."

Swinging her into his arms again, he carried her up the stairs into her bedroom and gently placed her on the bed.

"I'll talk to Beloff about our holiday in the morning," she whispered. "I'm sure he'll let me go."

"If he doesn't, you can tell him it's what your doctor ordered!" She laughed and he stopped the sound with his lips and then drew back at once. "Goodnight, Briony. I'd better go while I still can."

The communicating door closed behind him and Briony stood up shakily and began to undress. Had she dreamt the scene that had just taken place, or had it really happened? The brightness of her eyes and the deep red of her lips told her it had been no dream but a reality which had to be faced, which she had never believed would happen again. Yet it *had* happened. Without her knowing it she had fallen in love again. Head bowed, she sank on the bed and wondered how and when it had happened. She had despised Daniel, hated him for his determination to be a success no matter what it cost him. Even a few short days ago she had felt the same way about him, though by then she had conceded that his great ability as a surgeon went some way to mitigating his enormous ambition. But that she should love him. . . . Yet love him she did. It was as if his kiss had unlocked the gates that had imprisoned her, releasing the emotion she had held in check since the night Christopher had callously told her he was engaged to another girl.

Had she fallen in love on the rebound? Had she turned to Daniel because his strength could give her the ballast she needed? This was the logical answer, but she knew it was not logic that made her love this enigmatic man. Not that he would remain enigmatic for long. Soon they would be alone together and he would allow her to see behind the barriers he had built around himself to the inner man. She hugged the thought close as she lay in bed, wishing she were able to hug Daniel himself but appreciating his understanding in not taking tonight what she so willingly wanted to give him. Loving Daniel would be demanding, requiring not only her ardour but her tenderness. Close to him she would teach him not to be afraid of loving; not to be afraid of total commitment.

"Daniel." She whispered his name aloud like a benediction, and with a faint smile on her lips fell asleep.

# CHAPTER NINE

RUNNING into the breakfast room next morning Briony was disappointed to find that Daniel had already left the house. Pouring a cup of coffee, she chided herself for being upset that he had not left her a note. He was a mature man with the responsibility of life and death on his hands. It was foolish to expect him to act like a lovesick schoolboy.

She was still telling herself this when she reached the theatre, but once rehearsals got under way she was too busy to think of anything except the new ballet.

"You seem very happy," Neil Halper remarked as he lifted her up above his head and gently set her down again. "Anything nice happened?"

"It soon will. I'm going on holiday with my husband."

Neil gave a start of surprise and Briony wobbled, bringing forth an irate shout from Beloff which set both dancers on their mettle again.

"No more talking," Briony pleaded. "I don't want to put Oleg in a temper!"

"Even if he's as sweet as sugar, he'll explode when you tell him you want to go away. He'll never let you."

"Then I'll walk out. I haven't had a holiday for two years."

Arms aloft, she pirouetted to the far corner of the room and paused there while Neil completed a short solo. Glancing at Oleg's face, she decided not to talk to him until this afternoon when he might be in a more relaxed mood. Would she really leave the company if he refused to let her take a month off? Astonishingly she knew she would. There was no question as to what came first in her life as there had been when she had believed herself in love with Christopher. Her future with Daniel was so important that she would have no compunction

121

in giving up dancing if this was what he wanted her to do.

"How did the wedding go?" The question came from Ann Fielding, the only girl in the company whom Briony counted as a friend. "Tell me all about it over lunch."

Sitting in the green-painted canteen, Briony did so, her mention of George Leonadis bringing round-eyed wonder to Ann's face.

"Hobnobbing with the rich, aren't you?" she whistled. "How about getting him to endow a theatre for us?"

"The neurological wing comes first."

"I suppose that's a better cause," Ann grinned.

"There's no suppose about it. We can easily do without ballet, but we can't do without hospitals."

"Quite the little defender of the knife, aren't you!"

Briony blushed, realising this was the first time she had defended Daniel's actions. Thinking of his determination to get the neurological wing built, she remembered that this was why he had forced Christopher to marry Maureen. It was the only one of Daniel's actions she could not condone, and she knew that the sooner she discussed it with him the better. Tonight she would ask him to tell her the story from *his* point of view. Christopher had lied when he had said Daniel had threatened to make life difficult for his stepmother unless he went ahead with his marriage to Maureen; and if he had lied about this, it was more than likely he had done so about everything else. It was amazing how naïve she had been to take Christopher's word.

"Telephone for you, Briony," a young man with blond hair called out from the doorway. "It came through to the stage door."

Briony raced to take the call, certain that it was from Daniel.

It was, and hearing his voice so calm and confident, her bones seemed to melt with love for him.

"I'm so sorry I missed you this morning, Daniel. I rushed

down, but you'd gone."

"I left earlier than usual. I didn't want to wake you up."

"I wish you had." Now that he was a disembodied voice she lost her shyness with him. "I hate going through a day without seeing you first. We must share a bedroom and you can use the other one for dressing." There was no reply and she regretted her impulsive remark. "Are you – are you still there?" she asked nervously.

"With my secretary."

Instantly she understood. It was stupid of her not to have guessed he had someone else in the room.

"I'm flying to Cape Town in an hour, Briony," he continued. "Roger Morrison was injured in a car crash and they want me to operate."

Astonishment held her tongue captive.

"I'm sorry to spring it on you like this," he went on, "but the call came without any warning."

"I see." She found her voice at last. "Can I – can I go with you?"

"Go with me?"

"Yes. I wouldn't be able to catch the same plane, but I could follow you out tonight."

"It wouldn't be worth it. I'm not likely to have much free time while I'm there. I'm sorry about it, Briony. It means we'll have to postpone our holiday."

"As long as it's only a postponement," she said, instantly happy again.

"You didn't think I was cancelling it indefinitely?"

"I wasn't sure."

"I'll have to put that right as soon as I can." He spoke in measured tones, as though he did not want his secretary to guess the importance of the words.

"Will you be away long?"

"A week, perhaps. I'll certainly have to stay for seventy-two hours after the operation."

"Can I come and see you off?" she pleaded.

"There's no time. I'll be on my way to the airport in five minutes. Goodbye, my dear. Take care of yourself."

Fighting back the tears, she put down the receiver. There was no need to ask Beloff for her holiday now. She might as well wait until Daniel came back.

Driving home that night she was restlessly aware of Daniel flying further and further away from her, and her thoughts lay on her face as she entered the drawing-room before dinner, and drew sympathy from Mrs Clayton.

"What a shame about Daniel having to go to Cape Town. Still, he shouldn't be away for long."

"So he said." Briony perched on the arm of a chair and idly swung one slim, firm-muscled leg. "I suppose he's used to flying around the world like this?"

"Not so much now. He went to Beirut last year – some oil sheik had a brain tumour. But most of his patients come here to see him. And he certainly won't go traipsing off once he has his own wing."

"Then we must get it built as quickly as possible," Briony smiled. "Let's arrange that dinner for Mr. Leonadis as soon as Daniel gets back. He didn't think he'd be away longer than a week."

"Deirdre will do her best to keep him as long as she can," Mrs. Clayton said.

"Deirdre?"

"Deirdre Morrison, Daniel's ex-fiancée. You remember I told you about her."

Briony's leg stopped in mid-swing. There was a rushing sound in her head and for a moment she was incapable of speaking. Mrs. Clayton did not seem to be aware of the bomb-shell she had dropped and was contentedly working at her petit-point. Questions burned on Briony's lips, but she knew she had to be careful how she asked them. When Mrs. Clayton had first told her that Daniel had been engaged she had done so in the belief that Briony already knew of it. To appear curious might be dangerous. She must go on pretending she had always known about the girl.

"Did Deirdre know Roger Morrison when she jilted Daniel?"

"Oh yes. They met when he came to England for a holiday. He made it pretty obvious he wanted her." The needle flashed in and out of the canvas. "He wasn't a picture-book hero, you know. If it hadn't been for his millions you wouldn't have given him a second look. But once Deirdre knew Daniel meant to spend two years in Canada, she decided to settle for money."

"I bet she regretted it once Daniel became a success."

"I'm sure she did. She came to England a couple of years ago and I know Daniel saw her a few times."

"I can't see him playing second fiddle to another man," Briony retorted.

"I don't think Deirdre wanted him to do that. She came here to dinner and made it obvious she would divorce her husband if Daniel said the word."

Briony stared fixedly at the carpet.

"Why didn't he? After all, he – he hadn't fallen in love with *me* yet."

"What a silly question," Mrs. Clayton laughed. "Surely you know how moral Daniel is? He'd never dream of taking another man's wife!"

"But if he still loved her. . . ."

"I don't know whether he did by then. He never spoke of it. He took her out while she was here and then she suddenly returned to Africa."

Briony's leg started to swing again as more questions crowded in for answers. Had Daniel refused her offer to fly out to him because he didn't want her to meet the woman he had once been going to marry?

Abruptly she jumped up. "I'm hungry and the gong's

gone." She bent to help the older woman to her feet. "While Daniel's away, why don't we have dinner up here? Or, better still, Fay and I can have it in your room and you could stay in bed."

"I won't have you make an invalid of me." Mrs. Clayton moved purposefully into the hall, almost colliding with Fay who was coming in.

"Isn't it a nuisance about Daniel flying off like this?" Fay linked her arm with her sister. "He was going to take me into hospital tomorrow. Did he tell you about it?"

"He told me you spoke to him," Briony answered. "I was going to talk to you about it later."

"There's nothing to talk about." Fay looked at Mrs. Clayton's departing back. "For the first time in years I did the right thing."

"What decided you to tell him about the necklace?"

"I didn't want him to go on thinking badly about you. If he knows how wonderful you've been to me – that you aren't capable of doing a mean thing even if your life depended on it – I'm sure he'll fall in love with you!"

Briony chuckled, her mood of sadness lifting. "What an incredible romantic you are!"

"What's wrong with that? If you could only forget Christopher –"

"I forgot him ages ago."

"Then perhaps you and Daniel will –"

"There's no perhaps about it," Briony interrupted again. "Daniel was waiting for me when I came home last night and we – we talked about a lot of things. We're going away for a holiday together as soon as he comes back from South Africa."

"How wonderful!" Fay flung her arms wide. "I could jump for joy!"

"Don't try it till you come out of hospital!"

Fay was instantly motionless. "Do you honestly think

Daniel can help me?"

"He'll bring in the best people he can."

"So did Tom."

"Daniel may have other ideas too."

"I think he has. He admitted last night that he's been watching me since I've been here. He said that –" Fay stopped and shook her head. "Let's not talk about it any more. It makes me nervous.'

Together they went down to the dining-room where Mrs. Clayton was waiting for them.

"I think it's high time you both called me Sylvie," she said as they came in. "I feel so ancient every time you call me Mrs. Clayton."

"I like the name Sylvie," Fay grinned, sitting down and picking up her soup spoon. "Isn't it peculiar to have three women dining together like this? I feel as if I'm at boarding school!"

"I'll ask Tom to come over one evening," Briony suggested. "I'll call him and see when he's free."

Tom came to dinner on Thursday – his usual free night – and the three of them dined in the breakfast room, for Sylvie decided to remain in bed.

"This is the life of Reilly!" he exclaimed as the butler walked out with the first course. "Hard to think Daniel ever pigged it the way I do."

"I'm sure he didn't," Fay answered. "He's always had stacks of money!"

"He didn't use any of it in Canada," Tom replied. "When he was working with the professor he lived with him in two rooms and did the cooking for them both!"

"You're joking," Briony said, half questioningly.

"Scout's honour I'm not! Genius often goes with madness, and I gather the old professor had a touch of both. He liked his personal life to be stark and simple." Tom helped himself to another roll. "Have you heard from Daniel since he left?"

"No. I don't suppose he thought it worth phoning. He might even be on his way home now."

Briony doubted this even as she said it, but was glad she managed to hide her disappointment that Daniel had not called her. Had she not known Deirdre Morrison was his ex-fiancée she would not have found his silence unnerving; as it was, she could not help feeling jealous and apprehensive.

Dinner over, they went to the drawing-room, where Briony sat by the fire content to leave Fay to entertain Tom. Her sister had always been able to make him laugh, but now they seemed to be talking more seriously, and from the occasional sentence she overheard she knew their conversation was not medical, but an animated argument on the latest exhibition at the Tate Gallery. Fay, it seemed, did not like Leger – whom Tom did.

"Come with me on Saturday and I'll see if I can improve your appreciation of him," he was saying.

Fay stuck out her tongue at him and he lunged forward as though to pull it. "The last girl who did that to me –" he stopped, the freckles standing out on his face.

"Well," Fay prompted, "what happened to her?"

"She got well and truly kissed. Like this." He pulled Fay towards him and proceeded to do so.

Briony stared at them, seeing the stupefaction on her sister's face. It was a look reflected on Tom's, and for several seconds the two people on the settee remained motionless, as though caught in time. Incredulously Briony knew she was witnessing the beginning of a new intimacy between them. No longer were they doctor and patient; neither were they friends, but man and woman awakening to the potential of a new relationship.

Casually she stood up. "If you don't mind I'll go to bed. Can you see yourself out, Tom?"

"I'll go now if you like."

"There's no need," Fay murmured. "*I'm* not tired."

128

"Then I'll stay," Tom said quickly.

At the door Briony hesitated again. "If it's your weekend off, Tom, why not spend it here?"

His face glowed though he spoke with gravity. "Bit silly to do that. I'm only half an hour away by car."

"It would still make a change for you. Think of it as your luxury hotel from Friday night to Sunday!"

His hesitation merely paid lip service to appearance, and Briony hid a smile as she went out. But the smile disappeared when she was alone in her room, and dejectedly she undressed and climbed into bed. It was ridiculous to miss Daniel so much. He had only been gone five days and their life together had not yet even started.

The burr of the telephone brought her heart into her mouth, and she trembled with joy as she answered it and heard his voice in her ear.

"I hope I haven't woken you up," he said.

"No, I was just lying in bed thinking about you. What are *you* doing?"

"I've just left the hospital." His voice was strained. "Morrison died an hour ago."

"Oh, Daniel, I'm sorry!"

"It was hopeless from the beginning," he told her.

"So it was a wasted journey for you?"

"There was always the million to one chance."

"Of course." She changed the subject. "Will you be home for the weekend?"

"No. That's why I'm ringing. Deirdre – Morrison's wife – has taken it badly and she's asked me to stay on for a while."

"Doesn't she have any family?"

"A brother in Brazil, but they've never been close."

Briony longed to ask Daniel how close Deirdre considered that he was, but prudence kept her careful. "What about Luther's?"

"I've already checked with them and it's all right. There

are certain advantages to being a senior consultant," he added dryly.

She could not hold back the next question. "How long will you be away?"

"Another week at least. Deirdre's badly shocked. She was in the car with Morrison when it crashed."

"Was she hurt too?"

"No. She came out of it without a scratch. That's why she feels so badly."

"I see." Briony made her voice as loving as she could. "I'll miss you, Daniel – very much."

There was silence and the line crackled loudly. "I know how you feel," he said above the noise. "I'll try and call you again next week, but if you don't hear from me, don't worry. I might be tied up. Take care of yourself."

With the conversation over, Briony felt as let down as though he had not called her at all, and she jumped out of bed too agitated to remain still. There had not been one single word of affection in anything he had said. He could just as easily have been talking to his secretary. She wandered over to the dressing table. Roger Morrison was dead and Deirdre was free. The danger of the situation could no longer be ignored. The woman Daniel had once loved was not tied to another man. She could marry Daniel; she could now share his life, his work, his love.

But he loves *me*, Briony thought. Yet he had never said so; never put it into actual words. Even the knowledge that he wanted to make their marriage a real one gave her surprisingly little comfort, for he had not known that within a few hours of saying so to her, Roger Morrison's unattainable wife would become an attainable widow.

Desperately she tried to remember everything Daniel had said to her the night before his departure. If she had not been so tired that evening she might have had something more to remember him by than a few kisses. Yet they were all she had to remember, and she clung to the memory of them, striving to believe they had been a declaration of love and not just the result of passion held too long in check.

But the fear that might not be anything more than passion was an agony that made sleep impossible, and she paced the floor for hour after wakeful hour. She was Daniel's wife and this was her home. He was only being kind by remaining in South Africa for another week. He would have done the same for anyone. Anyone.

"I've no reason to be jealous about," she said aloud. "Once Daniel's home everything will be fine."

# CHAPTER TEN

It was two weeks before Daniel returned to England. He had telephoned Briony once again, but his words had been so stilted that she had been certain he had been calling from Deirdre's home – possibly with his hostess within earshot. Longing for a word of affection from him, she was hurt that he had not made sure he could talk to her in private, or even find the time to send her a letter, and her voice had been so cool that he had immediately asked if anything was wrong. But her reply that she was missing him had elicited no affectionate response, and her belief that he was being overheard had become a certainty. Which had made the rest of their conversation even more stilted.

But now Daniel was in England; his telegram giving his time of arrival being delivered almost as his plane touched down at Heathrow. She wondered why he had not given her more notice so that she could have gone to meet him, and put it down to his reluctance to display his feelings in public. Because of this she waited for him at home, feverishly hoping he would arrive before she had to leave for the theatre.

For the last few days she had not danced at all and it was ironic that on the night of his return, she was appearing for the first time in *Spectre de la Rose*.

At six o'clock Daniel had still not returned, though a call to the airport told her that his plane had long since arrived. Could he have gone to the Luther Hospital first? The thought made her smile; it was just the sort of thing he would do. At a quarter past six she was unable to wait for him any longer and, bitterly disappointed, she left for the theatre.

During each interval she waited expectantly for a call from him, but none came and she resisted the urge to telephone him instead. The weeks of his absence had made her more aware of him than if she had seen him each day; forced to live on memories, she had relived all the conversations she had ever had with him, seeing them afresh in the light of her love for him, and realising how easy it was to misjudge a person. Though she understood him better now, she knew there were still depths that she could only plumb with his help.

It was unfortunate that *Spectre de la Rose* was last on the programme, and it was nearly midnight before she returned home. There was no light in the library and with a nervous gesture she pushed back a strand of hair and ran swiftly up the stairs. But both bedrooms were in darkness and she came out on to the landing again and saw Fay peering down at her over the banisters.

"I've been waiting up for you, Briony. Daniel got back half an hour after you left."

"Where is he?"

"With Deirdre Morrison."

Briony was glad her sister was too far away to see her face clearly. "You mean she came back with him from South Africa?"

"Yes. That's why he was late getting here from the airport. He took her to her hotel first."

"Where is he now?"

"When he knew you wouldn't be home till late, he went back to Mrs. Morrison's hotel. She's at the Ritz," Fay gave a dry laugh. "It's exactly the place to suit her. Very ritzy she is!"

"You mean you've seen her?"

"Daniel brought her here to dinner – all pale and beautiful in black chiffon." Fay limped down the stairs. "You'd better tart yourself up, old girl. You've got stiff competition."

"I don't believe in competing for a man. If he doesn't know his own mind he's not worth having." Briony made an effort to pull herself together. "Anyway, you're talking rot. Mrs. Mor-

133

rison's just been widowed and —"

"She's got her sights on Daniel," Fay interrupted. "A blind man could see it!"

"Daniel isn't blind."

"You'd be surprised how many men are — where women are concerned!"

"You've been reading too many melodramas," Briony said and, feigning a yawn, kissed her sister goodnight and went into her bedroom.

She didn't even bother with the pretence of trying to sleep, and she was still wide-eyed and wakeful at two o'clock when she heard the door of Daniel's room open. Nervously she waited for him to tap on the dividing door or perhaps to open it quietly and see if she was awake. But the only sound was the opening and closing of a couple of drawers and then silence.

Briony's longing gave way to anger. How could he return home after weeks away and not even tiptoe into the room to look at her! Tears trickled down her cheeks and turning her head into her pillow she wept quietly and bitterly.

In the morning, with no early class to attend, she deliberately remained in her bedroom, willing Daniel to come in and see her before he left for the hospital. But there was no sign of him, and peering from behind the curtains she watched him leave the house and get into the car. Only then did she get dressed, filled with a lethargy that made her movements heavy. What had gone wrong between Daniel and herself?

The question gnawed at her all morning, and she was glad when afternoon came and she was forced to attend her practice class.

Halfway through it Oleg Beloff called her over. "I'd like you to dance Giselle," he said abruptly. "You've understudied long enough. It's time you tested the audience's reaction."

"When?" Briony asked, pretending to an elation she did not feel.

"Friday night."

"So soon?"

"Since you were ten years old you have been waiting for the chance!" Beloff exclaimed. "And when I give it to you, you say so soon!"

She smiled at his comment and was rewarded by a sharp glance. "Put ballet first and your husband second," he advised. "In that way you will be happier."

"And when I'm too old to dance?"

"By then the need for a man won't be so strong!"

Returning home, Briony wished she were old already. At least the pain caused by Daniel's behaviour would not affect her so badly if she were! As she walked up the steps to the front door she saw lights on in the library. Her heart gave a leap of joy. He had come home early to see her. Everything was going to be all right. Without giving herself time to think she ran across the hall and into the library.

"Daniel!" she cried happily, and then stopped as she saw he was not alone.

Standing beside him, so close that her skirts were touching his leg, was a tall, slim woman. Working in a profession that attracted beautiful girls, Briony had to admit that the one in front of her could have beaten them all. She looks the way *I* should, Briony thought, and stepped forward.

"Hello, Briony." Daniel took her hand but made no attempt to kiss her. "I'd like you to meet Deirdre Morrison."

"How do you do?" Briony said formally, and felt as if she were being taken apart and put together again with computer speed by almond-shaped green eyes.

Everything about Deirdre Morrison spoke of money and taste, from her careful make-up to the simple black dress whose soft material stopped sufficiently low to display the gleam of skin at the shoulder line and the entire length of her slim arms. Her black hair was pulled away from her face and lay glossy and curling on the nape of her neck, held there by a narrow gold circlet studded with tiny diamonds. Diamonds sparkled in the lobes of her ears and the hand held out to Briony was weighed down by an enormous marquise. For such a recently bereaved widow she appeared remarkably poised, and looking into the oval face Briony knew she was meeting a woman whose only thought was for herself. Fay was right. Here was an enemy to be feared.

"I hope you'll forgive me for keeping Daniel away from you for so long?" The voice fitted the face: cool, charming yet distant. "But I'd never have managed without him. He was so capable, he took command of everything."

"You had a whole retinue of solicitors who would have done the same," Daniel interposed, sounding embarrassed. "I didn't stay to look after your affairs, Deirdre, but to look after *you*!" He glanced at Briony. "Can I get you a drink?"

Conscious of her lack of make-up and workaday jumper and skirt, she shook her head. "I'll go up and change first." She looked at Deirdre, uncertain whether or not to say good-bye.

"Deirdre's dining with us," Daniel said, interpreting the look.

With a faint smile Briony left the room and had just reached her bedroom door when Daniel called her name. She turned to see him beside her.

"I tried to telephone you twice at the theatre today," he said, "but my secretary kept getting the engaged signal."

Joy slowly seeped into her, but she still kept her manner cool. "She must have been phoning the box office instead of the stage door."

"I never thought of that! I just asked her to get you at the theatre." He hesitated and looked at her hand on the door knob. "May I come in with you for a moment?"

Wondering why he was acting like a stranger, and fearing it was because he regretted what he had said to her the night before his departure to South Africa, she nodded in silence. Though he had only been away a couple of weeks the position between them now was entirely different, for today the girl he had once loved was free. No longer would she have to leave her husband in order to be with him, and the gossip that the divorce of a wealthy man would arouse was no longer something to be feared. But none of these thoughts were on Briony's face as she led the way into her bedroom, though nerves made her speak, and she said the first thing that came into her head.

"Why didn't you tell me Mrs. Morrison was your ex-fiancée?"

"I didn't think it was necessary."

"How odd. Surely you knew I'd be interested that you were going to see the girl you might have married instead of me?"

"I went to South Africa to try and save a man's life. I didn't stop to think whose."

"But you knew you'd be seeing Deirdre. That's why you didn't want me to come with you!"

"Don't be ridiculous. I told you I'd be too busy."

"I'm sure you were." She sat down in front of the dressing table and began to brush her hair.

"I'm sorry I didn't tell you about Deirdre," he said quietly, "but I've never found it easy to talk about my private affairs."

"Not even to me?"

Their eyes met in the mirror. "Particularly to you. Until the night before I left for Africa we were hardly the best of friends."

"But *that* night . . . why didn't you tell me then?"

"I was thinking of other things."

The words brought a blush to her cheeks, but they didn't reassure her, for he was talking about desire and she was talking about candour.

"How long is Mrs. Morrison staying here?"

"I don't know. She has no particular reason to return to South Africa. It will probably be better for her if she doesn't." He crossed his arms on his chest. "As I told you, she was in the car when it crashed and she feels guilty that she wasn't killed too. Particularly as. . . ." he stopped, and then continued: "Particularly as earlier that evening she had asked Roger for a divorce."

"I see!" Briony set down her brush and looked at it as though she had never seen one before.

Daniel walked over to the window and then away from it. "They weren't happy together. Deirdre didn't love him. Morrison knew it, of course – she told him so before she married him – but he said it didn't matter. Unfortunately it *did* matter to him. Once they were married he became obsessed by her." He hesitated again. "She was extremely unhappy."

"She stayed with him six years," Briony said.

"She wouldn't admit her mistake. But eventually she couldn't stand it and asked for a divorce. He suggested they went for a drive to talk things over – apparently his intention was to kill them both."

"Oh no!"

Daniel nodded. "He crashed the car and Deirdre was flung free."

"And now she *is* free – in every sense." Briony stared Daniel fully in the face. "When she asked for a divorce, did she know you were married?"

"No," he said slowly, and the way in which he answered her question gave the answer to the one she had not yet asked.

"So she wants to marry *you*?"

He nodded.

"You must feel flattered," Briony said bitterly. "After jilting you six years ago she suddenly realises her mistake. Or was she waiting until you were rich and famous before she left her husband?"

"Don't be childish! You asked me a question and I answered truthfully. Now let's forget Deirdre and talk about us. The night before I left England. . . . What did it mean to you?"

"Mean to me?" she repeated, wondering why he needed to ask such a foolish question. Didn't he know the answer without having to be told?

"Was it only desire?" he went on abruptly. "The need to be loved because you were lonely and unhappy that Christopher had finally gone from your life?"

She went on staring at him, incredulous that he could think Christopher still mattered.

"It was the night of my brother's marriage," he continued. "Were my arms replacing *his*?"

The hurt caused by his accusation was so strong that emotion made it impossible for her to speak. But even as she struggled to reassure him she suddenly saw another reason behind his question.

"Is that what you want me to say, Daniel? That I only responded to you because of loneliness?"

"Why should I want you to say it?"

"So that you can run back to Deirdre with a clear conscience!" The knowledge of the beautiful woman waiting for him downstairs; of the two weeks in Africa without a loving word from him, and his strange behaviour since his return all signified the truth of what she was saying and goaded her into saying more. "Don't try and turn me into your scapegoat. Go back to your rich widow, if that's what you want. I don't give a damn! Not one single damn!"

For a long moment there was silence. Then he spoke, his voice unexpectedly soft. "Thank you for your honesty. It will make things much easier for us both."

He walked from the room and Briony swung round on the stool and lowered her head on the dressing table.

The training required to be a ballet dancer came to her aid that evening and at seven-thirty she was in the drawing-room wearing a dress she had bought expressly for Daniel's homecoming and which – though his homecoming was not as she had envisaged – she deliberately wore. Simply cut, with a tight-fitting bodice, billowing sleeves and full, swirling skirt, the grey chiffon made her look as ethereal as a will-o'-the-wisp.

"What a lovely dress," Sylvie remarked as Briony came into the drawing-room where she was already talking to Daniel and Deirdre. "You should wear grey more often. It makes your hair look the colour of a toffee apple!"

Fay echoed the comment and stayed close by her sister's side, a gesture of support which Briony felt in need of as the evening progressed.

"I didn't know you collected Chinese porcelain," Deirdre exclaimed to Daniel as she took her place at the dining table. "Roger had some wonderful pieces. I'd like you to have them." He smilingly refused the offer and Deirdre shook her head at him. "Don't be so stuffy, Daniel. If you don't want them I'll just give them away to other people. I couldn't bear to auction any of his possessions, but I can't go on living with them either. I want to begin afresh – with everything new and my whole life starting again." She looked directly at Briony. "I feel like Sleeping Beauty waking up to find that all the horrid things have been a dream and that I've got my whole life ahead of me again."

It was a skilful allusion and, giving credit where credit was due, Briony knew that if it came to verbal sparring she would be left far behind.

"When is Christopher coming home?" Deirdre asked Daniel. "I'm looking forward to seeing him. Is he still a breaker of hearts?"

"Maureen will break his head if he is!" Sylvie Clayton said. "She won't stand any nonsense from him on that score!"

"What an unusual way for a mother-in-law to talk," Deirdre laughed.

"I know my son."

Briony glanced up and saw Daniel's eyes fixed on her face. Thank heavens he believes I'm still in love with Christopher, she thought. It was far better for him to think *that* than to know she had been stupid enough to fall in love with *him*.

"How long are you staying in England, Deirdre?" Mrs. Clayton voiced the question uppermost in Briony's mind.

"I've no idea. I'll probably settle here."

"Didn't you make any friends in South Africa?"

"Roger liked to keep me to himself." Deirdre's face became more beautiful as sadness settled on its classic features. "He couldn't even bear it if I favoured any of the servants." She sighed. "I still can't believe I'm free – that I can do anything in the world I like. The only thing that bothers me is that I don't feel his money should be mine."

"But you were his wife," Fay said.

"I was going to leave him. I'm sure he'd have changed his will if he'd had the chance."

"Give the money away, then," Fay said with asperity. "Then you won't suffer pangs of conscience!"

"How clever you are!" Deirdre looked artlessly ingenuous. "That's exactly what I'm going to do. Not all of it, though. Just enough for Daniel to build his neurological wing."

"A wonderfully generous thought," Daniel said into the stunned silence. "But I've no intention of accepting such an offer."

In the distance a telephone rang and the butler came in and looked at Briony.

The call was from Beloff. Jacqueline, who was supposed to dance *Spectre de la Rose* tonight, had been taken ill with food poisoning.

"You've an hour to get here and change," he commanded "Leave at once."

"I'm on my way," Briony replied, and rushed back to the dining room to explain.

"Marriot will drive you," said Daniel.

"I can take a taxi."

Without answering he signalled to the butler, who immediately went out, and when Briony ran down the front steps a few moments later, the limousine was waiting for her. Never had she been so glad to return to the theatre as she was to-night. Even though she knew she was leaving Daniel alone with Deirdre, she realised there was no point fighting the inevitable. As soon as he deemed it wise he would suggest a quiet annulment of their marriage and thus another chapter in her life would end. But this chapter was not going to be so easily forgotten. If only she had taken Beloff's advice and made the ballet her life.

It was midnight before she arrived home again, and as she crossed the hall to the stairs the library door opened and Daniel and Deirdre came out.

"How tired you look," the woman exclaimed. "Do you often have to rush off at a moment's notice?"

"This is the first time I've done so."

"I suppose you love it. I mean ballet is a dedication of one's life, isn't it?"

"It's the only thing I care about," Briony lied vehemently.

Deirdre looked taken aback by the remark and then gave Daniel an amused look. "Do you mind taking second place to an entrechat, darling?"

"Not at all. Briony and I are both dedicated to our work." He glanced at Briony. "I'm driving Deirdre back to the Ritz."

"I hope you don't mind," Deirdre apologised to her. "I promise not to keep him long."

"He isn't yours to keep at all!" Briony retorted coolly, and walking past them both, went up the stairs.

Anticipating that she would lie wakeful until she heard Daniel return, Briony surprised herself by falling asleep the moment her head touched the pillow, and she did not awaken until after eight o'clock next morning.

Deciding not to bother with breakfast she dressed, put on her coat and ran downstairs. Only as she closed the front door did she see Daniel about to step into his car, and seeing her, he waited until she came abreast of him. In his heavy coat he appeared to tower over her and she wished she had worn high heels instead of flat, childish pumps.

"I'll give you a lift," he said.

Something in his attitude decided her not to protest, and she obeyed him. Sitting next to him, the glass partition separating them from Marriot, she was aware of his unfriendly glance.

"I hope you regret your rude outburst of last night," he said. "It's childish to insult Deirdre. Until I flew out to Cape Town she had no idea I was married."

"Did she still think you were pining for her?"

"Does it matter what she thought?" His anger became puzzlement. "From the moment I got back you've been different. Is it because I tried to make love to you before I went away? I promise you it won't happen again."

Hurt tightened Briony's throat and, unable to speak, she stared fixedly through the window.

"You're very quiet," he murmured at last. "And pale too. You're not ill, are you?"

"Just working too hard."

"You need a holiday." There was a pause. "I don't suppose you'd care to go on the trip we talked about before I went away?"

"Isn't that rather unnecessary?" she said sharply. "You only suggested it then because we – because you. . . ." She forced herself to continue. "People often turn to each other when they're lonely. They say things they don't mean, do things they regret. If –"

"You needn't go on," he interrupted. "I quite understand. But as I had made the offer, I wanted you to know I'm still willing to keep it."

"It's very kind of you," she said brightly, "but even if I wanted to accept I couldn't. With a new ballet to do, it's impossible for me to get away."

"You were going to do so."

"I'm afraid I wasn't thinking clearly." She forced herself to look at him. "You're a good lover, Daniel. You made me forget –"

"Christopher?"

She caught her breath. "If I stop making remarks about Deirdre, do you think you could stop referring to your brother?"

"By all means. It's more civilised to have a truce until. . . ."

He didn't finish the sentence, but Briony was only too well aware that she could do so for him. A truce until convention allowed Deirdre to discard her widow's weeds and triumphantly proclaim herself his.

"I'm taking Fay into hospital tomorrow," he said abruptly. "There are various tests I want to do on her."

"What sort of tests?"

"You wouldn't be any the wiser if I told you!"

"But –"

"Stick to ballet," he said dryly, "and let me be the doctor in the family!"

The words momentarily warmed her, making her feel as if they were a unit. But even as the thought came into her mind, she discarded it, glad to see the massive bulwark of the Luther Hospital ahead of her, and knowing that soon she would be in the car alone, without any need to hide her tears.

# CHAPTER ELEVEN

FAY went cheerfully into hospital and Briony accompanied her there, intrigued to see inside a world which was so much a part of Daniel's life.

An unending stream of nurses came in to make sure Fay was settled, at the same time taking a good look at Mr. Clayton's wife.

"You must feel as if you've married a god," Fay giggled as the twelfth nurse departed. "Considering the way they practically faint at the sound of Daniel's name, I'm surprised he isn't more bossy at home!"

"He doesn't need to be. He gets his own way without it!"

"What about the holiday you were going to have with him?"

"It's been scrapped."

"Because of Deirdre?" At Briony's nod Fay banged her hands on the counterpane. "He's crazy! I was so sure he loved you."

"Perhaps he thought second best was better than nothing. But now Deirdre's free. . . ."

"Has he actually said this to you?"

"He made it quite obvious."

Fay's reply was forestalled by Daniel's entry. It was the first time Briony had seen him in the hospital and though he wore a dark navy suit which she recognised, there was an air of command about him, increased by the obsequious way in which the Floor Sister hovered by his side.

"You needn't stay while I'm with my family, Sister," he said, turning to her. "This is a purely social visit."

The Sister gave a smile and bustled out, and Daniel stood by the foot of the bed, arms akimbo, his stance so familiar that Briony knew she would never be able to see any other man do it without remembering this one.

"I'm beginning your tests right away," he said to Fay. "Some of them may be a bit uncomfortable."

"I won't mind so long as you cure me!"

"I make no promises," he reminded her.

"I was teasing you," Fay said quickly. "But this is the last time I'm coming into hospital. If you can't help me, no one can."

"I appreciate your faith." He glanced at Briony as he spoke. "If you're ready to come home I can take you."

"I'm going to the theatre."

"You're not dancing tonight again, are you?"

"I'm meeting Sebastian Browne. He's doing the costumes for the new ballet."

"I see. In that case I'll go on alone."

Not until he had left the room did Fay look at her sister with irritation. "Aren't you going to put up any fight for him?"

"I don't believe in fighting for a man. And don't let's talk about it any more. I can't bear it."

The house in Cumberland Terrace seemed inordinately quiet with Fay in hospital, Christopher still honeymooning in Bermuda and Daniel either at the hospital or preoccupied with Deirdre. His prolonged absences eventually caused his stepmother to remark on them, the first time she had made any critical comment about him to Briony.

"You shouldn't let Deirdre have all her own way," she said half jokingly. "If something is worth having it's worth keeping."

"One has to have it first."

"But Daniel loves you," Sylvie said slowly. "I'm sure of it. And you love him. You didn't when you were first married, but you do now."

"You're very observant," Briony said uncomfortably.

"Because I'm concerned for Daniel's happiness. I don't

146

know why you've quarrelled – and I'm not prying – but I beg you not to give him up so easily."

"Maybe *he* wants to give *me* up." Deciding it would be less embarrassing to tell Sylvie the truth about her marriage, she gave a monitored version of the reason for it, omitting Christopher's name entirely, but saying Daniel had met her at the theatre and had seen her as an ideal hostess for the social life he intended to pursue.

"He felt I could help him to raise the money for the neurological wing," she concluded, "and he thought I was going to make my name as a ballerina – which would add to his standing."

Sylvie burst out laughing. "Daniel didn't mean a word of it! You surely don't think he needs a ballerina to add lustre to his name? Honestly, my dear, he's turned down marriage to an Italian princess, an English countess and –"

"Because he still loved Deirdre."

"But he married *you*."

"Still loving Deirdre," Briony persisted. "He knew he'd never forget her, so he decided to marry me as the next best thing. He said himself that I wouldn't make demands on him and that by providing Fay with a home he'd guarantee my behaviour."

"You don't believe that!"

"I only know he doesn't love me," Briony reiterated.

"Well, I'm positive he doesn't love Deirdre. She wrote to him several times last year saying she wanted to leave her husband, and if Daniel had loved her, wouldn't he have agreed?"

Briony shook her head. "It would have meant an unpleasant divorce and scandal."

"Deirdre wouldn't have let herself get involved in a scandal. She'd have got a divorce in a way that would have put her in the best possible light. The fact that she didn't leave Roger Morrison meant she wasn't sure if Daniel wanted her."

"But she did ask for a divorce – that was the reason for the accident."

"We only have Deirdre's word that she did – and I wouldn't believe her if she swore on the Bible, the Koran and the Talmud!"

Faint hope stirred in Briony, but not sufficient to give her any reassurance.

"Don't you love Daniel at all?" Sylvie asked suddenly, and immediately looked stricken. "I shouldn't have asked that. I'm sorry."

"Don't apologise. I wouldn't pretend with you. I love him very much. I knew it the night before he went to South Africa."

"Did you tell him?"

"Not in so many words. I thought he had guessed it. But when he came home I realised he hadn't. He thinks I – I still love another man."

"He must be blind. You light up like a lamp when he comes into the room!"

"Men only see what they want to," Briony said ruefully, "and Daniel would find my loving him an embarrassment."

A commotion downstairs prevented further conversation and she stood up to go and see what it was. But before she could do so, Christopher and Maureen came running into the room.

"Darlings!" Mrs. Clayton cried. "You're two days early!"

"We got homesick for England," Maureen grinned, and turned to Briony. "You and Daniel were far more sensible to start your married life at home. It's much nicer than staying in a hotel and being gawped at by everyone because you're newlyweds!"

"It never embarrassed *you*, monkey face!" Christopher laughed, and met Briony's gaze with an ease he had never shown before. "Where's Big Brother?"

Briony was saved from replying by Mrs. Clayton, who said:

"With Deirdre Morrison," and then went on to relate all that had happened in the past few weeks.

Briony tried not to listen, and instead focussed her intention on Maureen, who was looking exceptionally happy. So was Christopher. Indeed they both had the same aura of relaxation. With a start she saw that a package was being held up to her, and that Sylvie was untying a similar one to disclose an exquisite bedjacket.

Forcing herself to look enthusiastic, Briony unwrapped her own gift, her delight becoming genuine as she saw a chiffon nightgown, its variegated shades of amber reflecting her colouring.

"I chose it," Maureen said. "Christopher wanted to buy black!"

"I didn't," he exploded, and then shamefacedly admitted: "But I did suggest red!"

Briony laughed and moved over to kiss Maureen.

"What about me?" Christopher said, and gave her the same enveloping hug he had given his mother.

Briony's reaction to his gesture reaffirmed her belief that she no longer loved him, and looking at him she realised she must have seen him with Fay's adoring eyes, and been bemused by his talk of all he could do for her sister. She glanced at Mrs Clayton and saw a yawn being hidden quickly.

"I think we'll leave you to rest, Sylvie," she suggested. "We'll go down to the drawing-room."

Once settled in the elegant lower room, Maureen announced that she wanted to talk to her parents, and blowing Christopher a kiss she left him and Briony alone together.

The atmosphere remained relaxed, though it grew less so as she became aware of his speculative gaze.

"Has Daniel been starving you, or are you on a diet?" he asked finally.

She shrugged. "I've been rehearsing for the new ballet and it's very strenuous."

"You're used to that sort of work. It wouldn't make you look so haggard. What's wrong? I know you too well to let you get away with excuses like that."

"Since when have you known me so well?" she asked lightly, and was surprised to see him give the question serious consideration.

"What I should have said is that I know *myself* better. And *that* helps me to know other people." He stared at her. "You're unhappy, Briony. It's written all over you. And it's not because Fay's in hospital. There's more to it than that."

"You're imagining things." She jumped up and drifted round the room, her graceful movements making her look as though she were floating.

"What do you think of the lovely Deirdre?"

The question was unexpected, and she stopped dead. "I – I don't know her very well. She doesn't bother to make friends with women!"

"You know she was once engaged to Daniel?"

Briony nodded and sat down again, unaware that her hands were shaking until she saw Christopher's eyes focussed on them.

"Are you unhappy because of Deirdre?" he asked.

"Don't be silly. I hardly know her."

"But she knows Daniel – too well. Is that why you look like a walking corpse? You haven't gone and lost your heart to my unloving brother, have you?"

"Don't be crazy!" she said again. "You know I – I can't stand him. I wish I'd never met him."

"So you hate him, then?"

"Of course not," she retorted angrily, and bit her lip as she saw Christopher smile. "Don't build up an emotion that doesn't exist," she went on. "Daniel means nothing to me. I don't hate him and I – and I don't love him."

But no words could still the shaking of her body or the wild fluttering of the pulse in her throat, and the look on Christopher's face grew more thoughtful.

"You poor sap," he said bluntly. "You *do* love him." The blond head tilted. "I take it he doesn't know?"

She nodded, accepting the futility of lying. "You mustn't tell him. He must never know."

"So you sit here with Mother while he consoles the bereaved widow and —"

"Regrets he ever married me," Briony finished. "But at least he can't blame *me* for his marriage – only you."

Christopher looked surprised. "What did I have to do with it?"

"You can't have forgotten already?" she said wearily. "Daniel married me to make sure you didn't change your mind at the last moment about Maureen. He knew that if I was *his* wife you'd go ahead and marry her."

There was a long silence, broken finally by Christopher, who said, "Oh, lord!" several times in varying tones of unease. "So you still think that," he said finally. "I was hoping you'd guessed the truth." He hesitated. "Did Daniel actually tell you that was his reason for marrying you?"

She thought for a moment. "I said it. But he didn't deny it. He told me that I –"

"That you must believe what you want to."

She was surprised. "How did you know?"

"Because that's the sort of thing he would say! As a kid, when he used to cover up for me and Mother suspected it and asked him, he always gave that as his answer!"

Briony knew she was expected to find some clue in this remark, but she was too emotionally worn out to do so, and she looked at Christopher helplessly, so that he gave another unhappy sigh.

"I've behaved like a swine, Briony, but I'm afraid you only know the half of it." It was his turn to pace the room. "Daniel never forced me to marry Maureen. I made it up. He wouldn't have cared if I'd married the dustman's daughter! *I* was the one who wanted to further my career – and I chose Maureen because she could help me – through her father."

"Sir Geoffrey could help Daniel too," she persisted.

"Daniel didn't need me to marry Maureen for her father to push the Board into building the neurological wing. They had decided to do that months ago. It was merely a question of raising all the finance. And *that* was only a matter of time: six months – perhaps a year before the project went ahead. That's why I wanted to marry Maureen."

"I don't understand."

Christopher ran his hand through his hair. "For heaven's sake, Briony, I'm an architect! I work with a good firm, but I'm struggling to make a name for myself. If I were put in charge of designing the new wing for Luther's. . . . Don't you see?"

Her expression told him she did, and he reddened. "Now you know what sort of swine I am. When I met you I fell for you like a ton of bricks, but I knew all along that I could never marry you. I tried to stop seeing you several times, but. . . ." He hesitated. "Maureen was inclined to be self-sufficient and you and Fay were good for my ego. You made me feel needed. I'm not trying to excuse what I did," he added, "I'm just hoping you won't judge me too harshly."

But Briony was too preoccupied with thoughts of Daniel to judge Christopher at all. "Then why did your brother marry me?" she whispered.

"To help Fay, I suppose. If someone is ill and he thinks he can help them, he'll stop at nothing."

"He could have helped Fay without marrying me."

Christopher's look was contemplative. "I fell for you the minute I saw you. Perhaps he did too."

"Not the first time," she said emphatically, remembering how she had looked and what he had thought of her. But could he have fallen in love with her later and knowing at the time that she was still in love with Christopher – have been unwilling to tell her how he felt? It made sense, and the more she thought of it the more credible it became. Yet his behaviour to Deirdre remained unexplained and she said so.

"Perhaps Daniel's using her as a cover?" Christopher suggested. "I've already told you he's got the devil's own pride. If you want to find out if he loves you, *you'll* have to make the first move."

Maureen's return made the conversation turn to more general topics, and Briony was relieved when they finally drove off to their new flat.

At once she went to her room to apply fresh make-up, using rouge to hide her pallor; then downstairs again to the library where she switched on the lamps and moved the curtain apart so that Daniel could see the light when he came home.

It was nearly midnight before she heard his key in the lock. His steps crossed the hall, hesitated and then the library door opened.

"I thought you'd be in bed," he said quietly. "Is anything wrong?"

"No. Christopher and Maureen are back. They got homesick."

He made no comment and went on looking at her in his usual impassive way.

"I waited up because I wanted to see you," she continued, and nervously moved to the other side of the room where she was protected by shadow. Her grey chiffon skirts melted into the dimness and only her pale face and tawny-coloured hair gave away her presence. "I found out tonight that Christopher was lying when he said you'd forced him to marry Maureen." She paused, hoping Daniel would say something. But when he didn't, she knew she had to continue, and wondered bleakly if he was determined to extract his pound of flesh for the way she had disbelieved him. "He admitted he wanted to marry her for his own ambition. That it had not had nothing to do with you. I misjudged you, Daniel. I'm sorry."

153

"Sorry?"

She flung out her hands. "I should have had more sense. I should have known you weren't the sort of man to force anyone to do something because of your own ambitions."

"Obsession, you called it."

"Don't remind me," she said quickly. "I said so many cruel things to you."

"Forget it. *I* have." He sighed. "I realise how hard it must have been for you to tell me, and I appreciate it. I'm glad you no longer think me such an ogre."

He was not making it easy for her to continue, yet she could not blame him. Her eyes blurred with tears and she took an uncertain step towards him. "You don't know how badly I've felt since I heard the whole story. When you love someone desperately and then find you've been wrong about them. . . . Oh, Daniel!"

"It won't always be so painful." The harshness of his voice startled her. "I let you go on believing what you did about me because I didn't want to destroy your illusions about Christopher. I knew you'd eventually discover the truth, though I must say I didn't think he'd have the courage to tell you himself. At least that's one good point in his favour."

"I know."

"And you'll forget him in time. I can promise you that. No love is so great that you won't eventually get over it – particularly you, with your talent and a wonderful career ahead of you."

"But, Daniel, you don't understand." Tears flowed down her cheeks and she gulped as he came towards her with a handkerchief to wipe them away. The white linen was crumpled and as he raised it she saw the lipstick mark on it. Deirdre's lipstick.

Horrified, she backed away from him. Thank heavens he had misunderstood what she had said. One day he might think about this conversation and realise what she had been trying to

154

tell him, but for the moment he was still mentally too close to Deirdre; physically too, she thought bitterly, and looked at his handkerchief again. How dared he try to comfort her in this physical way when he had come straight from Deirdre's arms?

"I'm going to bed," she whispered. "Goodnight, Daniel."

"Thank you again for apologising," he said abruptly, and turned to his desk as she walked from the room.

Briony found solace in work, and Beloff was delighted at her willingness to go on rehearsing with him and Neil long after everyone else had gone home. To her surprise the costumes and scenery for the new ballet suddenly appeared and a full-scale rehearsal was called. It was strange to work on the stage instead of in the drab practice room: strange to feel diaphanous folds of material around her as she and Neil danced. Frequently Beloff stopped them while props were moved from one position to another, and occasionally the wardrobe mistress was called to give her comment when a costume did not fall in the way he wished, or when Briony or one of the other dancers complained that they found their movements restricted. As always many things had to be altered, though the choreography itself was left untouched, and she began to appreciate the hours of toil to which Beloff had subjected them.

Unusual for him, he called an additional rehearsal for Saturday, a day when they normally did not come to the theatre until the matinée. But he seemed determined to have Neil and Briony do another full-scale rehearsal, and after they had finished he showed them a printed synopsis of the story and the title which, until this moment, he had kept a secret.

"I am calling it *Mermaid and Fisherman*," he said. "It is simple, but it says enough."

"When's the first night?" Neil asked.

"I haven't decided."

"Don't tell me," Briony shivered. "The thought of it gives me goose pimples."

"You are quite ready to dance it," Beloff retorted irritably. "Do not let me hear you talk such nonsense."

He strode off and Neil grinned at her. "He's right, you know. This is our big chance, Briony. If we foul it up we've had it."

"We won't foul it up," she said with more confidence than she felt. "That's part of Oleg's technique. He makes you dance the same thing again and again until you know it in your sleep."

"You make him sound like a sadist."

"He is," she smiled, "but then we're masochists! We wouldn't be ballet dancers otherwise!"

On Sunday Briony spent the day in hospital with Fay. Since the night of Christopher's return she had not seen Daniel alone, and she knew she would not be able to go on living with him for much longer. If it weren't for Fay she would have left him already, but she could not do so without her sister finding out, and at this moment Fay's peace of mind was more important than anything else.

In the afternoon the small room was filled with visitors. Christopher and Maureen dropped by for half an hour; several of the girls from the company appeared and Tom arrived with a large bunch of flowers and grapes.

"Hello, ugly," he said, ruffling Fay's hair. "How are you feeling?"

"Fine," she said gaily. "I've been examined by three different surgeons, and I can't for the life of me imagine what's going to happen next."

Fay went on chattering, but looking at Tom, Briony had the feeling that he already knew. However, it wasn't until he took her out for a snack at supper-time that she had a chance to ask him.

"Daniel wants her to have an operation," he said. "I'd like you to talk to him."

"But you're our doctor. You tell me."

156

"Daniel's not just the specialist in the case. He's your husband. I'd rather you spoke to *him* about it."

Alarm stirred in her, but Tom refused to be drawn, and after returning to the hospital to say goodbye to Fay, she went home.

It was too early for Daniel to have left the house; on Sundays Deirdre lunched at Cumberland Terrace, went back to the Ritz for tea and rested there till eight, when he collected her again.

Briony now went in search of him. He was not in the library as she expected, nor in the drawing-room, but as she entered her bedroom she heard him next door, and, after a moment's hesitation, she knocked on the panelling. He opened the door and she saw that he was wearing his dressing gown.

"I'm sorry, Daniel. I didn't realise I was disturbing you. But I've spoken to Tom and I'm worried."

"About the operation?"

"Yes, Tom said you'd tell me about it."

He rubbed the side of his jaw. "It's a dangerous one. Very delicate and difficult. But she must have it. If she doesn't, she'll get considerably worse."

This was something Briony had not anticipated and her scalp prickled. "You mean she'd limp more?"

"Not only limp," he said slowly. "But her moods – her depression – would increase."

Again he rubbed the side of his face, giving the impression that he had something to say but did not know how to say it. Forgetting her embarrassment at his nearness, she stepped closer to him.

"Fay says you've brought in three different surgeons to see her. Who's going to operate?"

"I will."

"You? But you're a neuro-surgeon!" She frowned. "I thought Fay would need an orthopaedic man."

Daniel's hand came out and led her to a chair. "Sit down,"

he said gravely, and waited till she had done so before taking a chair opposite her. As he relaxed the collar of his dressing gown rolled forward and she saw the dark tangle of hair on his chest.

"Fay has a tumour on the brain," he said bluntly. "She may have been born with it. The fact that she's limped since she was a child suggests it. It's developed slowly, but in the last few months not so slowly. That's why you've noticed these swings in her moods and why the pills she took didn't help her."

Briony swallowed. Her throat seemed restricted, but she knew it was only nerves. "You said the operation was a delicate one. *How* delicate?"

"It depends how deep the tumour is and whether or not it's malignant. If it is, the operation will only – only delay her death. But if it's benign and we can remove it, she'll recover completely."

It was several moments before Briony could speak, "There's no choice, is there? Fay has to have the operation," and even when she did so, her voice was thin and shaking with fear.

"Yes." There was no lightening in his mood as he stood up. "If you'd prefer someone else to operate, I can recommend Christoffson."

"I want *you*. If you can't succeed, no one can."

"I'm human," he said harshly. "Remember that!"

As if she would ever forget it! Avoiding his eyes, she stood up.

"When will you tell Fay?"

"Tomorrow. I'd like to operate the day after."

"So soon?"

"The sooner the better," he said grimly, and went back to his room.

It seemed to Briony that traumatic events in her life never came singly. On Tuesday Fay would be having a life-and-death operation, and on Friday she herself was dancing Giselle, the culmination of ten years of effort and work.

Worry for her sister swamped all personal pleasure, and mid-morning on Tuesday she left the practice room and went to the hospital. Beloff had suggested she did not come in at all that day, but hoping she could sublimate her fears by dancing she had not accepted his offer. Yet she had found it impossible to concentrate and, still in black tights and sweater, her face denuded of make-up, she went to Luther's and waited tensely in the private patients' waiting-room. Several times one or other of the nurses came in to see her, but though she accepted coffee she was unable to eat anything.

"It will be several hours before there's any news," a staff nurse told her. "An operation like this can take five or six hours. Why don't you go for a walk?"

"I'd rather wait here."

"I understand how you feel, Mrs. Clayton, but your sister couldn't be in better hands."

Remembering those long beautiful hands, Briony nodded. "Is Dr. Bristow in the theatre too?"

"Yes. He was in Miss Stevens' bedroom when she had her pre-med and he went down with her to the theatre."

Glad that Fay had been able to see Tom's face until the last moment of consciousness, she knew how much she would long to see Daniel's face if she were in a similar position. Yet within a few days, whether the operation was a success or not, she would leave Cumberland Terrace and never see him again. Once before she had vowed to put a man from her life and concentrate on her work, but the vow had lasted a matter of weeks and she had fallen in love again with a depth of feeling that would not allow her to forget so easily.

No matter what the future held, Daniel would always have a place in her heart. No fame that she achieved would ever eradicate the knowledge that she would have given it all up willingly to be his wife and the mother of his children. Tears poured down her cheeks and she was glad that the nurse had left the room. Angry that she should be crying for herself instead of Fay, she wiped her eyes and thought about her sister, remembering the good and bad times they had shared, and praying that the good times would return again.

# CHAPTER TWELVE

SLOWLY the hours ticked by. At one o'clock the staff nurse returned with more coffee and some sandwiches which Briony forced herself to eat, and at two o'clock, when she was wondering how she could bear the suspense any longer, the door opened and Daniel came in. His face was grey with fatigue and made his eyes look startlingly green.

"The tumour was benign," he said without preamble. "But the next twenty-four hours are critical from a general point of view."

"Do you think she'll be all right?"

"Are you asking me as Fay's surgeon or as her brother-in-law?"

"As both."

"As her surgeon I can only repeat what I've just said, but as her brother-in-law. . . ." He gave a faint smile. "I'd say that by this time next week you'll have a bald-headed but perfectly normal sister nagging to be let out of here!"

With a cry of joy Briony flung herself into his arms. Light though she was, the impact jolted him and he put his hands around her to steady them both.

"You're wonderful," she choked. "Oh, Daniel, I love you!"

She clung to him, her arms round his neck, her cheek pressed against his. She was aware of the thick springing hair beneath her hands and the faint smell of ether.

"All grateful relatives love the successful surgeon," he said lightly and, untwining her arms, set her away from him. "You should go home and rest. You look ready to collapse."

"So do you."

She was amazed that her voice could sound so calm when she was still stinging from his rebuff. How could she have let

161

emotion carry her away in this stupid fashion? From now on she must be careful what she said. It was the second time she had told him how she felt and the second time he had misunderstood her. The third time she might not be so lucky, and then she wouldn't even have pride to give her courage. But for the moment she did have pride, and she drew it around her like a cloak and tilted her head.

"I'll wait and go home with you, Daniel. I rather like seeing the envious stares of the nurses!"

He looked startled. "As you wish. But I won't be ready for another hour."

"I'll wait," she said, and sat down again.

It was only when she was walking beside him down the corridor some half hour later that she realised how incongruous she must look in her simple navy coat and flat-heeled shoes, her legs encased in black tights and her hair knotted carelessly away from her face. And what a face, she thought. Skin white as a ghost, eyes seeming twice as large in a heart-shaped face whose cheekbones stuck out too prominently – a sure sign that she was far too thin. No wonder Daniel still regarded her as a child who hankered after his big blond brother. Yet she was a child who stood between him and the woman he loved. Anguish shot through her and she stumbled. Daniel's hand steadied her, his arm so strong and comforting that she clung to him as he half led, half carried her to the lift.

"You're still pining for Christopher," he said harshly. "That's why you don't eat! Why you've got no strength. Where's your will-power, Briony? Start your life again. Fall in love with another man. There are plenty around who would make you an admirable husband."

"When I'm ready I'll ask you to find me one!" She pulled away from him. "In the meantime leave me alone. I wish I never had to see you again!"

"That's one thought I endorse."

162

The lift door slid back and he made an effort to take command of himself as they emerged into the reception hall and went out of the hospital to the limousine and Marriot. Not until they were together in the back did she speak again.

"What you just said – about not wishing to see me. . . ." She took a breath. "I'd already made up my mind to leave you, but I wanted to wait till Fay had her operation."

"I'm glad you showed *some* sense." He paused. "Where will you go? You gave up your flat."

"I'll find somewhere else by the time Fay comes out of hospital."

"She'll need careful nursing for several months."

"I'll make arrangements."

"She could stay at Cumberland Terrace for a while," he said.

Until he was married to Deirdre, Briony supposed, and resisted the urge to turn round and hit him; to do anything that would provoke him into showing some feeling towards her. Yet what difference would it make if he kissed her in anger? Those sort of kisses were as unwanted as kisses of passion without love.

"Your offer is very generous, Daniel. I'll accept it."

"That's sensible of you. You can always come and see her during the day when I'm at Luther's. Then we won't need to meet."

She said nothing and they were still silent as they reached the house. Not for several weeks had Briony been home to lunch, and as she entered the hall she smelt the faint elusive perfume that told her Deirdre was here too.

"I didn't know Deirdre was lunching with us," she said. "Why didn't you tell me?"

"What difference does it make?"

"None." She walked past him up the stairs.

Defiantly she did not change for lunch, merely washed her hands, smoothed back her hair and went down to the dining-

163

room. Only as she saw Deirdre, beautifully dressed in pale cashmere wool, did she regret her decision, for the woman made no effort to hide her amusement at Briony's black tights and sweater.

"You look like a schoolgirl," she laughed. "I'd no idea you were so young."

"I'm twenty-two," Briony said quietly, and took her place at the head of the table. She looked at the butler with unusual command and signalled him to serve the soup.

"You look about fifteen. Doesn't she, Daniel?" Deirdre said.

"The reward of innocence," he replied.

Deirdre pouted. "Are you being nasty about *me*, darling?"

"I like sophistication," he smiled.

Briony concentrated on her soup, but as Daniel and Deirdre continued to talk in quiet undertones, her temper began to stir. She and Daniel might not have a normal marriage, but there was no reason why politeness should not be maintained. It was outrageous that she should be made to feel an interloper in her own home. For this was her home, she told herself. Daniel had asked her to marry him and she was still his legal wife.

"Are you enjoying your holiday in England, Deirdre?" she asked, determinedly coming into the conversation.

"I'm not here on holiday any longer. England is my home again now. Didn't Daniel tell you I'm buying a house in Eaton Square?"

"Daniel and I don't talk about you when we're alone, do we, darling?"

Daniel swallowed hard and Deirdre gave him a cool glance before she spoke.

"I wouldn't be happy living in South Africa any more. And now I'm free I want to be with my – with the people I love."

"I know how you must feel," Briony replied. "I'd hate to be away from Daniel. We missed each other terribly when he was in South Africa."

Daniel set down his spoon with a clatter. "Could you stop discussing our passionate feelings towards each other and ring the bell for the next course? I've got to get back to the hospital."

"Sorry, dearest." Briony did as she was told.

The soup plates were removed and the entrée was served. It was eaten in silence, and conversation only resumed with the sweet, when Deirdre spoke about her house and how she intended to furnish it.

"I'm having it done by Peter Bardell. He's an absolutely fantastic decorator."

"I wouldn't like an interior decorator to do *my* home," Briony commented. "They make everything so impersonal."

"I'm quite sure I'll be able to add the personal touches."

"I'm sure you can," Briony said. "You're so clever at being personal."

"The coffee," Daniel said pointedly, putting down his spoon and fork.

Again Briony signalled the butler and looking at her uneaten meringue she felt her anger dissolve. Suddenly all she wanted to do was run away and hide. But she wasn't going to give Deirdre that satisfaction, and she remained in her position at the head of the table: an unwanted wife who looked like a fifteen-year-old urchin, but was a wife nonetheless.

"I'll drive you back to the hospital, Daniel," Deirdre said.

"Fine." He looked at Briony. "Are you coming back to the hospital?"

"Will I be able to see Fay?"

"She won't be conscious and she won't be allowed visitors — not even you — until tomorrow."

"Could I peep in at her?"

"I'd rather you didn't." He softened the words with a barely perceptible curve of his lips. "When I come home I'll let you know how she is. I suggest you go upstairs and rest."

Wishing he would do the same, for he still looked pale and

tired, she went to her room and lay down. Fitfully she dozed, not wakening up properly until the sky was dark. Glancing at her watch, she saw it was six-thirty.

What was the news of Fay? She sat up sharply and as she did so Daniel came into the room. Aware that she was only in her brassiere, she drew the sheet around around her shoulders.

"I've just woken up," she said nervously.

"I know. I came in before, but you were still asleep. Fay's doing well. Pulse and breathing good and temperature steady."

In her relief Briony let the sheet go, hastily drawing it up again as she saw the sharp smile on Daniel's face.

"You were far more revealing when you danced in *Daphnis and Chloe*," he said coldly.

"There's a difference between seeing a woman on the stage and in her bedroom," she remarked.

"I wouldn't have thought it mattered to a sophisticate like you."

"This afternoon you said I was innocent!"

"That was before your display of pyrotechnics at the luncheon table."

"Deirdre doesn't have a monopoly of wit!"

"Neither of you used wit. You were both merely sharpening your knives on me."

Briony could not help laughing. It was a spontaneous sound and she threw back her head like a child, the curving line of her throat beautiful to see.

"You've got a sense of humour, Daniel. I never realised it!"

Unexpectedly he strode out, banging the door behind him, and Briony knew a thrill of pleasure that she had finally pierced his calm exterior.

The following day she was allowed to see Fay. Her sister looked more like a marble statue than a girl, her skin yellowish, her head swathed in bandages. Briony did not stay more

166

than a few minutes, and as she walked to the lift the door opened and Daniel emerged, two young interns with him. He froze at the sight of her, then urging the two men to go ahead of him, he escorted her into the lift.

"I've just seen Fay," Briony whispered. "She looks like death."

"She had a long anaesthetic, you know. It takes time to recover from it. You'll find a marked improvement in her by tomorrow. But try not to see her too late in the evening. She must rest as much as possible."

"I can come straight here from my class. I'm not dancing in the evening until Friday."

"Isn't that unusual?" He spoke in such an indifferent tone that she was stung by it.

"It's not unusual at all. When you dance a big role for the first time it's important to be fresh. I'm doing *Giselle* on Friday."

One of his brows lifted in surprise. "So you're climbing to the top of the tree!"

"The first branch at least."

"Dancing *Giselle* is the *top* of the tree," he declared.

It was the first friendly remark he had made for a long while, and though she wished it could have been a more personal one, it at least showed he was still interested in her career.

They reached the ground floor and walked to the entrance.

"Where would you like Marriot to take you?" he asked.

"I don't need to trouble him."

"He's your chauffeur as well as mine."

"For as long as I remain with you."

"I was wondering when you were going to refer to that again."

"You could have brought the subject up yourself if you'd wanted to know when I was leaving," she said tartly. "I'd have moved into a hotel today, but with Fay on my mind and worrying about *Giselle* —"

"There's no need for you to rush away," he interrupted.

"I'll move out at the weekend. There's a couple of rooms going at the house where Neil lives."

"I'd prefer you to take a furnished flat. They're not hard to find."

"They are at the rent I can afford."

"I will pay the rent. You are my wife and I won't have you living in lodgings!"

"Worried what people might think?" she taunted.

His mouth set in a hard line and gripping her tightly under the elbow, he escorted her to the car. "I hope you have a suitable dress to wear for tomorrow."

"What's special about tomorrow?"

"Leonadis and his sister are dining with us. And some other people too."

She stopped in her tracks. "No one told me!"

"I asked Sylvie to arrange it last week. I did mention it to you," he reminded her.

She sighed, remembering he had. "I didn't realise it was so soon. It slipped my mind. Sylvie should have reminded me."

"I asked her not to until I was sure what was going to happen with Fay. If the news had been bad, we'd have cancelled it."

"Without telling me?"

"Naturally, or you would have had something else to be guilty about."

"Something else?"

"You already feel guilty for marrying me while you still love Christopher."

"Then you should feel guilty too," she flashed. "You still love Deirdre!"

He nodded, tight-lipped, and waited in silence as she got into the car.

"To the theatre, madam?" Marriot asked.

"Yes, please."

Paying lip service to convention, she waved goodbye to Daniel, then sat back as the car moved through the crowded streets. How typical of him to make sure he arranged the party for Leonadis while she was still living at Cumberland Terrace.

Hard on this thought came a far more unpleasant one. Why did Daniel need Leonadis's money when Deirdre had made it obvious she would be delighted to give him whatever he needed? Or didn't he wish to be financially obligated to the woman he loved and eventually hoped to marry?

"Don't you get tired of practising, madam?" Marriot's question came as a welcome interruption.

"Never." Even as she spoke, she knew it was not true. She *was* tired of practising – and of dancing too. Tired of the whole egocentric world of ballet; the choreographers and designers; the petty jealousies and trivial arguments that could blow into a thunderous storm. How far removed it was from Daniel's world. But she was removed from his world too. At the moment, living in his house, she was still on the fringe of it, but once she left Cumberland Terrace she would know nothing more of his life. They would become total strangers.

"We are at the theatre, madam," Marriot said.

Not waiting for him to open the door for her, she smiled her thanks and ran down the short flight of concrete steps to the stage door.

A full-length dress rehearsal had been called for *Giselle*, and unexpectedly Briony gave an excellent performance, drawing applause even from the hardened *corps de ballet*.

"Tomorrow we'll rehearse it again," Beloff said, "and also *Mermaid and the Fisherman*."

"Not both together," Briony protested.

"The *Mermaid* only takes half an hour, and I want it to be fresh in your mind."

"The première's more than a month away."

He favoured her with a glare, and giving him a smile in return she ran off stage.

When Briony saw Fay the next day she was more reassured. Colour had returned to the waxy skin and her eyes were alert.

"It's been a success," Fay whispered, and gave a shaky laugh. "Apparently I wasn't to blame for all those horrible moods. It was something I couldn't help."

"I know, darling. But you won't have any excuse for being moody in future!"

"I don't think I ever *will* be. I feel as if I've been born again."

"I hope you'll make the most of it. You must fall in love and –"

"I already have. It's funny I never guessed it for so long."

"Tom?" Briony said.

"Are you surprised?"

"Not at all. I'm just delighted as long as *he* loves you!"

"He hasn't said it in words, but I'm sure he does. I feel it in my bones."

"Dem wonderful bones," a male voice quipped, and they both looked round to see Tom.

Fay coloured. "Shouldn't you be doing surgery?"

"I've got myself a locum for a few days. I decided I needed a holiday."

"Where are you going?" Fay asked in a small voice.

"To sit by the side of your bed! Being with you *is* my holiday, monkey face. But once you've stopped resembling a bald chicken we'll go off on our honeymoon!"

"Is this a proposal?"

"The only one I've ever made, my angel."

"I'm going," Briony said hastily, and blowing them both a kiss ran out.

Their obvious happiness highlighted the loneliness of her own future, but she forced her thoughts back to Fay, feeling an enormous sense of relief that at last she would no longer have to carry the burden of an invalid sister. If the operation had been done six months ago she wouldn't have had to accept Daniel's offer of marriage. Yet if he hadn't come into her life, Fay would still be lame – possibly even dying. She marvelled at his diagnostic acumen. If only it extended to the women in his life!

When she saw him again it was at dinner time and he was on his way out of the house.

"I didn't know Christopher and Maureen were dining here," he said, keeping his voice low. "Unfortunately I can't alter my arrangements. I hope you can manage on your own?"

"I'll try not to throw myself into his arms," she retorted.

His face tightened. "I suppose you imagine I find that remark funny?"

"Not half as funny as I find the image of *you* – in Deirdre's arms!"

His shoulders stiffened. "One day you'll try me too far."

"No, I won't. By this time next week I'll have gone."

Christopher and Maureen's arrival ended their tête-à-tête. Daniel apologised for having to dine out and left them, and Briony took over the role of hostess without any sign of the depression that was weighing her down.

Dinner was excellent as always, and Christopher kept his mother entertained with a long account of how he had tried to teach Maureen to water-ski.

"That's enough talk about *me*," Maureen said at last, and looked at Briony. "I can't wait to see you on Friday night. It'll be the first time I've seen you dance."

"Don't tell me you're finally managing to drag Christopher to a ballet!"

"No dragging was necessary. There's no point in having a famous dancer in the family if we can't bask in her reflected glory!"

"Daniel has booked a box," Sylvie said. "He's taking us all."

It was the first intimation Briony had had that the Claytons were coming to watch *Giselle,* and the knowledge that Daniel himself had made the arrangements filled her with puzzlement. He knew she was leaving him this weekend and it seemed strange that he should want to carry on the pretence of their marriage until the last moment; as strange as his decision to go ahead with his party for George Leonadis.

"How many people are dining here tomorrow?" she asked.

"Thirty. And every one of them with a title except the Leonadises and Deirdre – just as Daniel ordered!"

"He's a cunning devil," Maureen giggled.

"On the contrary – he's too damned honest," Christopher said with unexpected irritation.

"I wasn't criticising Daniel," Maureen protested. "You don't need to defend him."

"I know, honey. But now I'm an old married man I've stopped feeling like a jealous younger brother!"

Unable to bear any further discussion about Daniel, Briony signalled for coffee to be served in the drawing-room, and once up there, determinedly steered the conversation round to the house Maureen and Christopher were planning to build. By the time the evening ended she was exhausted with the effort of appearing gay and, once alone in her bedroom, fell asleep almost as her head touched the pillow.

It seemed a long time later that she sat up in bed with a startled exclamation. Something had woken her up. Steps in the next room told her what it was – the sound of Daniel's return.

Crossly she lay down again. Not normally a light sleeper, she must have been subconsciously waiting for him to come home, otherwise she wouldn't have awakened. She looked at her watch. Three o'clock.

He had spent seven hours with Deirdre. With an angry exclamation she buried her head in the pillows and burst into tears.

172

# CHAPTER THIRTEEN

KNOWING this would be her last dinner party with Daniel, Briony went out the next morning and bought the most elegant dress she could find. But putting it on that night in the solitude of her bedroom she wondered if bravado had made her go too far, for the dress was startlingly revealing. Not that it left her uncovered: rather it covered her in a way that left little to the imagination. Cinnamon brown chiffon draped itself round every curve of her body while a long slit in the skirt allowed for ease of movement as well as a tantalising glimpse of a silken-clad leg.

The unusual colour of the material accentuated the shade of her hair, which she had pulled free from its usual classical style to swing in a heavy cloud to her shoulders. Make-up transformed her pearly skin to a smooth, matt surface in which her eyes glowed with surprising brightness, framed by heavily mascaraed lashes whose slow lowering and lifting was a subtle yet sensual invitation. No fifteen-year-old waif to-night, she decided triumphantly, but a woman as brittle and beautiful as Deirdre.

The family were already in the drawing-room when she entered it, and for a moment she paused at the door, feeling very much Briony Stevens, the unknown little dancer. Then she pushed back her shoulders and walked forward.

"My dear," her mother-in-law said in the stunned silence, "you look superb!"

"Fantastic," Maureen agreed. "Doesn't she, Christopher?"

"And how! Something told me I shouldn't have brought my old lady with me tonight! Go home, Maureen, I've found the girl of my dreams."

He came forward, but Daniel stepped casually in front of him, blocking his way. Briony was certain he had done so deliberately, and for an instant she was puzzled. Then she realised that he thought she might be hurt by Christopher's flirtatious remarks. Incredible though it was, he was still trying to protect her.

"How do I look?" she asked him brightly, as he moved close.

"Different."

"Sophisticated and beautiful?" she asked.

"Extremely so."

"But not as beautiful as Deirdre, of course."

His mouth softened into a smile, but his eyes were looking past her, and with bitterness she swung round to see the woman she had been talking about. Still wearing black as a concession to her recent bereavement, Deirdre was breathtakingly beautiful in velvet and diamonds. They glittered around her throat and on her ears, and Christopher's off-key whistling of the Merry Widow Waltz as she came forward made Maureen and Briony turn away to hide their smiles.

Deirdre, however, fixed him with a haughty stare. "Darling Christopher – as bad-mannered as ever!"

"It's merely my brother's gauche way of saying you've bowled him over," Daniel said suavely and, in a gesture alien to him, raised Deirdre's hand to his lips.

Briony saw the startled look on Sylvie's face, but as the older woman's gaze met hers, she gave a brilliant smile to let her know that the gesture had not worried her in the least. Only two more days in this house and she would no longer have to pretend. If only Fay didn't have to stay here when she left the hospital. Yet it was an extravagance to take a flat that was suitable for them both in view of the short time they would be together. In three months – possibly less – Fay would marry Tom. Yet she could easily afford an expensive flat now that Beloff would be paying her a ballerina's fees. His announcement that he intended to do so from the beginning of the month would make a considerable difference to her income. If only it could compensate her for a life without a love! Yet that was something it could never do. Sighing, she looked at Deirdre. This was one instance when the best man had not won!

"Dear Briony, I'd never have recognised you," Deirdre exclaimed. "You look like a femme fatale."

"I'm sure you're well able to recognise the type!" Briony locked her arm through Daniel's and felt him stiffen at her touch. "I'm glad you could come to our party."

"Nothing could have kept me away." Deirdre focussed her limpid gaze on Daniel. "I understand you're giving the party in honour of George Leonadis? It wasn't a bit necessary, darling. If you want money from him —"

"I don't. I have the full amount I need."

Deirdre laughed disbelievingly and Briony silently echoed it, wondering why Daniel had bothered to lie. Ten days ago he had admitted he wanted money from the Greek. Why should he now say he didn't? There was no chance of asking him, for other guests were arriving, and within moments the room was buzzing with chatter and the clink of glasses.

Daniel kept Briony firmly by his side, introducing her to every new arrival until she was forced to protest that their guests had come here to meet Leonadis and not herself.

"They expect to meet you, too," he replied. "You're my wife and this is our first big party."

"And our last."

His eyes glittered green and hard, and she was uneasily reminded of the first time she had seen him, when she had thought what an implacable enemy he would make. But he had no reason to be her enemy any longer, and it was on the tip of her tongue to say so when George Leonadis and his sister were announced.

"George," Daniel said with pleasure, "I'm delighted to welcome you to my home."

"It has taken me weeks to be invited!" The Greek gave

175

Briony a conspiratorial wink, and realising she was expected to know why, she winked back and then smiled at his sister.

Almost immediately Deirdre joined them, standing so close to Daniel that she made Briony feel an outsider. "So you're George Leonadis," she purred. "I believe you once did business with my late husband."

"Indeed I did," the Greek nodded, and then succinctly explained that Roger Morrison had been the one man to best him in a deal. "I managed to extricate myself without a loss," he added, "but with none of the profit I had anticipated! After that I decided to give up mining and stick to shipping. Each man to his last, eh, Daniel? Me to ships and you to knives!"

"How gruesome!" Deirdre shuddered.

"How rewarding!" Leonadis corrected.

Dinner was announced and they went down to the dining-room where the long table gleamed with white linen and silver, crystal wine glasses glittered in the candlelight and delicate white china, rimmed with gold, marked each place-setting. Daniel and Briony sat facing each other in the centre of the table, with George and his sister as guests of honour. Top-heavy with titles, Briony expected the conversation to be sluggish, and was agreeably surprised to find it flowed as smoothly as the wine.

"You have an excellent cook," Leonadis said to Daniel. "Chryssoula and I spent the weekend at a country house last week – I won't tell you where – and we were so hungry we had to go out and buy some pork pies and chocolate to eat in our rooms!"

"George!" his sister said reproachfully, but her brother remained unabashed.

"What's wrong in being frank? It's what I am noted for! One of the nicest things about being rich," he added to Briony, "is that one can say what one likes. Few people have the courage to disagree with you or tell you you're wrong."

"*I'd* tell you," Briony could not help saying. "Money is no excuse for rudeness."

"Do you hear that, Daniel?" the Greek guffawed. "Your beautiful wife hates rudeness." He focussed his attention on Briony again. "What would you say if I told you that your husband was extremely rude to me on several occasions?"

"I'd say you were joking – or that you deserved it!"

"I am not joking," Leonadis insisted, highly amused, "nor did I deserve it, yet Daniel was extremely rude to me. And do you know what he did? He refused to invite me to his home!"

Briony half turned and saw Daniel watching her. There was an amused look on his face and she had the feeling he knew what was coming. She looked at Leonadis once more.

"I will tell you about it," he went on. "For many years I have wished for a title, and I soon realised the only way to get one was to give large amounts of money away to your English charities."

"You built a magnificent orphanage," Daniel interposed. "And you knew you wouldn't get a title for *that*!"

"The orphanage was nothing," the Greek shrugged. "I had a hard life as a child and I wanted to make life easier for a few other children. . . . No, the orphanage I built to please myself." His dark eyes shone full on Briony. "To get a title I knew I would have to donate money to a special cause, and then fate brought Sir Geoffrey into my life." He waved his arm to where Maureen's father was deep in conversation with Chryssoula. "He told me the Luther Hospital wished to build a neurological wing and that they needed half a million more. He introduced me to Daniel and I sat back and waited to be wooed." His laugh boomed out. "But nothing happened! After my first conversation with this husband of yours he went away and never got in touch with me again. And I," he said, waving his hand, "*I* had to contact *him*!"

"A good story, George," Daniel said hurriedly, "but no one believes a word of it. Let's talk about something else."

177

"And forgo a chance of embarrassing you? Never, dear friend! So," he went on to Briony, "I telephoned this most unfriendly Mr. Clayton and asked him why he didn't invite me to his home. And do you know what he said? That he never invited people to his home if he intended to ask them for money! So what could I do? I sent him a cheque at once and the next day I got my invitation!" He gave another hearty laugh. "And here I am at last."

Briony stared at him in astonishment. "You mean you've already – that my husband has got the money he needs?"

"Of course. I gave Sir Geoffrey three-quarters of a million pounds last week."

Only then did Briony look directly at Daniel. Why had he wanted her to believe he was only inviting Leonadis here in order to get money from him when he already had it? Did he want her to believe he was expedient? That his ambition over-rode everything else?

"You might have told me." It was Deirdre speaking, her voice furious. "*I* wanted to give you the money for the equipment – for my husband's sake," she added quickly. "Now I know why you kept putting me off."

"Luther's can always use money," Daniel said quietly. "If you wish to do something in your husband's name, I'm sure Sir Geoffrey will be able to advise you. I know he wants to modernise the children's block."

"I wanted the money to benefit *you*."

Daniel said nothing and Briony knew a thrill of triumph, though it faded quickly as she recollected her earlier thoughts on the subject. If he intended to marry Deirdre he might not wish to take her money. To do so would conflict with his need to be master in their marriage.

During the remainder of the evening she kept thinking of this, though her thoughts did not show on her face, and it was not until midnight, when the party broke up, that she questioned Daniel.

"Why didn't you tell me you had all the money you required? You deliberately allowed me to think you were only being nice to Leonadis because you were expedient."

"I thought you'd prefer to think badly of me!" His pale lids lowered and hid his eyes. "Go to bed, Briony. You have an important day ahead of you tomorrow."

"But —"

"Goodnight," he said.

Knowing herself dismissed, she swung round and ran from the room.

On Friday morning she remained upstairs until she heard Daniel leave the house. She was in no mood to continue sparring with him. All her energy must be conserved for tonight when she would be dancing one of the most arduous roles facing a ballerina.

At midday, on her way to the theatre, she went in to see Sylvie, who had also spent the morning in bed.

"Daniel made me promise I wouldn't get up till I had to get dressed for the theatre," the woman said. "Did he make you stay in bed too?"

"He can't make me do anything." Briony hesitated. She felt duty bound to say she was leaving Cumberland Terrace tomorrow, yet was reluctant to face the questions that she knew would follow her statement.

"What's wrong?" Mrs. Clayton demanded.

"I'm leaving Daniel. I won't be staying here after tonight."

"Oh, my dear, are you sure? Wouldn't it be better to wait?"

"Waiting won't change anything. Our marriage hasn't worked. The sooner we part, the sooner Daniel can start again."

"With Deirdre?"

Briony nodded, too close to tears to speak. Leaning forward, she kissed the grey-blonde head. "Wish me luck for tonight."

"I do, my dear. And I'm sure you'll be wonderfully successful. I only wish you had the same luck in your private life."

"After today I don't intend to have a life outside of my dancing. My future will be the ballet – nothing else."

On her way to the theatre she stopped at the hospital to see Fay. Even in a few days the change in her sister was miraculous. Her colour was normal and her eyes were bright and lively.

"Look what Tom bought me," Fay giggled, and pointed to a luxurious red wig on top of the dressing table.

Briony burst out laughing. "I think I prefer you bald!"

"I think I agree with you!" Fay caught her sister's hand. "I wish I could see you dance tonight."

"You'll have lots of opportunities for that. This isn't my farewell performance, you know."

"But everyone will be there tonight – except me."

"Stop feeling sorry for yourself. You've got so much to be thankful for. What does it matter if you miss me dancing *Giselle*? You're cured, darling. Think of that!"

Leaving her sister looking less pensive, Briony went on her way. She had deliberately not told her she was leaving Daniel this weekend. Time enough for her to know when it was a *fait accompli*. For the moment her sister must think only of getting completely well.

Entering the dressing room which Beloff had assigned to her, Briony had her first taste of stardom, for hardly had she closed the door when it was opened again by Bella, one of the company's most experienced dressers.

"I'm *your* dresser now," she announced. "If there's anything you want, let me know and I'll do it. Give me a couple of weeks with you, and I'll know what you want before you know it yourself!" She began to hang up the costumes she had been holding. "Would you care for a cup of coffee or tea, Miss

Stevens, or would you like to have a rest?"

"I've been resting for most of the day," Briony said, feeling suddenly hungry. "I'd like a cup of tea and a couple of buns."

The response brought another beam to Bella's face. "That's the kind of temperament I like," she said approvingly, and whisked off to return a few moments later with a pot of tea, several slices of warm toast and a plate of buns.

Briony was eating her second one when a bell-boy staggered in with an enormous bouquet of roses and orchids. A white card proclaimed them to be from Christopher and Maureen, and wished her success for tonight.

"That's what I call a bunch of flowers!" the dresser said appreciatively. "At least twenty quid's worth there."

"Don't be so mercenary, Bella!" Briony grinned. "People give what they can afford." She sat down at the dressing table and began to make up her face.

Almost as she did so two more bouquets arrived, one from Mrs. Clayton and the other from Fay and Tom. Resolutely she continued with her make-up refusing to think that the one person from whom she wanted to hear had not sent her anything.

Almost without her being aware of it, it was seven-fifteen. The orchestra could be heard tuning up in the pit and the house lights were on in the auditorium. Yet still there was no word from Daniel. Wearing her gay peasant dress, a wreath round her tawny hair, she remained in the dressing-room, and not until five minutes before the red velvet curtains were raised did she stand up to leave.

With a cardigan over her shoulders she walked to the crowded wings.

"You have nothing to be afraid of, Briony," Beloff said, catching her arm as she waited for her musical cue.

Repeating the words to herself as though they were a mantra given to her by her own guru, Briony moved out on to the stage and, pausing in the brilliance of the spotlight, found herself becoming Giselle. No longer was she a sad young woman pining for a husband who only had eyes for another woman. All at once she was a joyous peasant girl dancing with her friends and deliciously happy at the thought of the young boy she loved. Then tragedy came: the boy is found to be a prince in disguise – a prince who can never marry a village girl. Maddened with grief, Giselle began her dance of death, leaping and pirouetting as she pleaded with everyone to tell her that her lover had not deserted her, and that he would return to make her his wife. On and on the grief-stricken Giselle danced, only faltering as her heartbeats faltered, then dancing again before she finally fell, dying, in her mother's arms.

The curtains swung close, though it took Briony several seconds before she regained her composure and, with Neil by her side, stepped forward to receive the cheers of the audience. After the fifth curtain call Beloff motioned them to move back and, as they did so, he himself stepped on stage and began to speak.

Listening, Neil and Briony stared at each other in consternation. The rest of *Giselle* was not going to be performed. Instead the audience would be privileged to see the première of Beloff's ballet, *Mermaid and Fisherman*.

"You might at least have given us some warning," Neil said grimly as the man came off stage towards them.

"And have you both in a panic? That is exactly what I wanted to avoid. All the important critics are here – I made sure of that – and all you have to do is to dance the way you did the other day. Do that – both of you – and you'll have nothing to worry about."

As far as Briony was concerned Beloff's words were wishful thinking. Her limbs felt like melting jelly and she could hardly stand, let alone dance!

"It's impossible," she cried. "I can't do it. You'll have to get Davina to take my place."

Catching her roughly by the arm, Beloff pushed her along to her dressing-room where he ordered Bella to make some strong black coffee.

"You're wasting your time," Briony said through chattering teeth. "I can't dance half of *Giselle* and then go on and do the *Mermaid*."

She collapsed on to a chair and as she did so saw an enormous bouquet of freesias on the dressing-table. With a gasp she ran over to it, plucking out the small envelope that lay in the centre. Ripping it open, she took out a letter. It was from Daniel.

"I had hoped to bring you these myself before the performance, but I was delayed at the hospital. I wanted to make it red roses, but they didn't seem to be your kind of flower. Freesias *are*. Cool and pale; strong yet delicate-looking. I won't wish you luck for tonight – you've already had that from everyone else. Instead I wish you love – all the love you want – even though you do not want mine."

"What's the matter with you?" Beloff asked. "Why are you standing there like a ghost? You're not Giselle now. Come and drink your coffee."

As though mesmerised Briony did so. It burned her throat, warming her chest and stilling the trembling of her body. "I feel better," she said quietly, "but I'd like to be left alone."

Beloff glanced at Bella and then tiptoed out as though afraid of breaking Briony's mood of calm.

The moment she was alone she unfolded Daniel's letter again and read it. ". . . . I wanted to make it red roses, but they didn't seem to be your kind of flower. . . . I won't wish you luck for tonight . . . instead I wish you love – all the love you want – even though you do not want mine."

What did he mean? Red roses were for love, but surely he didn't mean he loved her? He was in love with Deirdre. Again she bent her head to the letter. "I wish you love – all the love you want – even though you do not want mine."

He couldn't mean what she thought. She wanted his love so desperately that she was reading things in this letter that weren't there.

"You'd better get ready, dearie," Bella said, unzipping Briony's dress as she spoke. "You've only got ten minutes."

Still chattering, she took out the Mermaid's costume, a glittering affair of green tulle and silver diamanté, and slipped it over Briony's head. The folds lay flat against her body, emphasising her slenderness and giving her an ethereal air heightened by the silver wig that fell like a ripple of water around her shoulders.

"A pity your sister can't be here to see you," said Bella.

"I hope she'll be well enough to come to the proper première." Briony was amazed her voice could sound normal when her thoughts were still trying to unravel the meaning of Daniel's letter.

"She's a lovely girl, your sister," Bella gabbled on. "If it hadn't been for that husband of yours she mightn't be alive today. A man like him deserves the best." She squeezed Briony's shoulder. "But he's got the best, hasn't he, dearie? He's got you!"

No, Briony thought, staring at Bella's thick features and kindly eyes. He's got Deirdre and she's far from the best. She only wants him because he's married to someone else. She remembered Christopher's assertion that Deirdre had never asked her husband for a divorce but had used the car accident to pretend she had, determined to make Daniel sorry for not having remained faithful to her. Yet Daniel *wanted* to marry Deirdre. He had said so. Not in so many words perhaps, but. . . .

"Believe what you want to believe." That was what he had said.

"Bella, help me!" she cried, and clutched the dresser's arms. "If someone you loved was going to make a terrible mistake, would you tell them they were wrong, even if you

184

knew they would be furious with you for saying it?"

"I've always been one to speak my mind," Bella answered. "You might be disliked for it, but at least you know you've done your best."

And the best thing I can do, Briony decided, is to try and stop Daniel ruining his life, even if he hates me for it.

"I want to write a note to my husband," she said, and pulled off a sheet of paper from a pad on the dressing-table.

The words scrawled across the page. "When we meet it will be impossible for us to talk alone. But I can't go out of your life without warning you not to make the same mistake I did. Don't love a dream. Face the fact that it doesn't exist. You are worth a hundred Deirdres. You lived without her before and I am sure you can do it again. I'm sorry you made a mistake choosing me as a replacement, but one day you'll find someone who will give you all the love you want – which Deirdre can never do."

"Ready for me to take it up, dearie?" Bella asked.

Briony nodded and folded the letter.

"Your husband must be so proud of you," the dresser went on. "Loving someone and knowing they love you gives a man strength. And dealing with life and death the way he does, he needs all the strength he can get."

Briony caught her breath. Strength. That was what Daniel needed in order to turn away from Deirdre. Yet she had never considered him lacking in strength. As a child he had never defended himself, Sylvie had said, and when blamed for something he hadn't done he had chosen to be thought guilty rather than have to assert his innocence. This did not imply strength but hurt pride. And someone who could be easily hurt needed the reassurance of knowing he was loved. Perhaps if Daniel knew how much she herself loved him he would find the strength to turn away from Deirdre.

Abruptly she appended a postscript to the letter. "Don't think I am unaware of what it means to love someone and yet know you have no future with them. I'm not referring to Christopher this time. What I felt for him was so childish and shallow that I can't believe I ever thought it was love. *You* are the fisherman in the ballet I'm dancing tonight, and I am sure that one day you'll find a mermaid of your own."

With the open declaration of her love for Daniel, it seemed as if a weight was lifted from her shoulders. She gave the letter to Bella, instructed her to give it to Daniel at once and then went to wait in the wings. What did pride matter when one loved someone so much that their happiness was more important than your own? Telling Daniel she loved him would not stop him loving Deirdre, but it might help him to put the woman out of his life.

The plaintive sound of violins echoed in her ears and there was instant quiet in the auditorium as the curtains glided back to disclose a battered fishing boat and a sailor fighting for his life in the storm. Drums rolled, cymbals clashed and the elements won as the sea claimed another victim. Behind masking gauze veils Briony took up her position, and as the veils lifted she was seen cradling the dead body of the fisherman. Desperately she tried to bring him back to life, running her hands over his chest and caressing his limbs. But he remained lifeless, and placing a ring of shells round him, she tried to entice him into life. But though she danced herself into exhaustion he did not awaken, and sobbing she fell at his feet. The swell of the sea grew louder as the gods took pity on the foolish mermaid and Poseidon himself came to tell her that if she gave up her own life he would give it to the fisherman. Without thought for herself the mermaid agreed, and amazed at the depth of her love Poseidon allowed her one night in the fisherman's arms.

The music changed, the lights dimmed momentarily, brightening to show the mermaid and the fisherman by the seashore, rocking gently together on the silver sand. A passionate pas de deux followed and the mermaid gave herself completely to the mortal, lying in his arms as the stars slowly faded and dawn lightened the sky. Only then did Poseidon return to remind the mermaid of her promise. In loving a mortal she had become human too, and her silvery scales scatter on the sand. But she had given her word to Poseidon. Her life for the life of the fisherman. Cradling the sleeping man in her arms, she kissed him goodbye and walked slowly into the sea.

As the curtains descended there was a hushed silence. Then applause crashed out, echoing round the auditorium like the very waves into which the mermaid had plunged.

Briony and Neil took endless curtain calls. The audience were on their feet cheering wildly, throwing flowers on the stage, shouting and clapping in a way that no one in the company could remember having heard for years.

Realising that both the dancers were exhausted, Beloff ordered the house lights up, but even this did not quieten the audience, and with the cheers still ringing in their ears, Briony and Neil gave a final bow. Only then did she turn to the box on the right of the stage, hoping that Daniel had gained courage from her message. But all she could see were two women and Christopher's blond head. Of Daniel there was no sign.

Tears poured down her cheeks and seeing them the audience clapped even harder. "Please," she gasped to Neil, "I can't take any more."

Arm around her, he led her off the stage where Bella rushed forward and draped a cardigan around her bare shoulders, while Madame Cassini teetered forward on high heels.

"Not bad," she said, though the tear marks on her cheeks indicated far more than her words. Briony burst into laughter, the sound seeming to come from a long way off, and Madame Cassini looked at her sharply. "Take her to the dressing-room," she ordered Bella, "and don't let anyone see her till she's calmed down."

"I want to be alone," Briony cried, and sped down the corridor.

The star on her door blurred into a thousand points through her tears and she turned the handle and went inside. Eyes closed, she leaned against the wall, regardless of the cardigan slipping to the floor.

"Put it on again," a calm voice said. "You'll catch cold."

With a gasp she opened her eyes and saw Daniel. Quickly she bent to retrieve the cardigan, but before she could do so he had lifted it up and placed it round her. Then he went to the door and turned the key in the lock.

"Not the ideal place for a discussion," he said, looking round the brightly lit room, "but it's better than not talking to you at all. And since our marriage, all we seem to have done is to talk at cross-purposes."

"I don't understand."

"I've heard that remark before too!" He led her over to the settee and pushed her in it. Then he sat beside her, close enough to touch her although he did not do so. "You are going to listen to me without interrupting."

"No," she gasped. "I don't want you to say anything. I should never have written what I did. I had no right."

"Didn't you mean what you said?" he asked sharply.

"No – yes. No," she said again.

"You don't seem very sure."

"I'm only sure of one thing," she whispered. "I don't want your pity."

"How about my love? If you don't want me to give it to Deirdre, I must be allowed to give it to someone else."

"Don't tease me," she cried, and gave a sob. "How can you be so heartless?"

"Because I haven't had a heart for months!" he burst out, quite unlike his usual calm self. "Ever since I met you in fact. Not the first night," he amended, "but the second time. When you came in from the theatre looking ready to drop on to the

188

floor with exhaustion. I wanted to take you in my arms and carry you away there and then. But I couldn't because you were the girl who loved my brother. The girl he had let down the way Deirdre had once let me down. . . . And while we're on the subject of Deirdre, which I'd like to get off as quickly as I can, let me say that I stopped loving her years ago. I was sorry for her when Morrison died and I tried to help her. But there was nothing more to it than that."

"You came back from seeing her with lipstick on your handkerchief," Briony said, refusing to look at him.

"She'd been crying and I gave it to her to wipe her face."

"Why did you let me believe you loved her?"

"Pride. The same pride that made you let me believe you still loved Christopher."

Still she could not take it all in. "You mean you've loved me all the time?"

"That's why I suggested we went away together! I thought if I got you to myself. . . ." He gave a sigh. "But then I came back from South Africa and everything seemed to go wrong."

"Because you came back with Deirdre. And because you were so unfriendly when you called me from Cape Town."

"I hate talking on telephones," he said quietly.

"You could have written."

"I didn't think you loved me. I believed it would take me a long time to make you see me as a man who needed you – wanted you – and not as someone who made you tremble every time he came near you."

"I trembled because – because I wanted you."

"Oh, darling," he whispered, and pulled her into his arms, cradling her against him the way she had cradled the fisherman. "I'd never let you drown for me, my dearest heart. You and I sink or swim together."

With a murmur she twined her arms around his neck and placed her mouth on his. In her diaphanous costume her body was as transparent as her feelings and Daniel's hands gently moved her away from him.

"We've waited so long," he said regretfully, "and it looks as if we'll have to wait a little longer. The family are meeting us at the Savoy."

"And afterwards you'll say I'm too tired," she whispered. "The way you did that other night."

"Tired or not, you won't sleep alone!" His lips were soft against her eyelids, his breath warm on her skin. "I won't be going to South Africa in the morning, my darling, just to Luther's to arrange that holiday I promised you!"

"Beloff won't –"

"He already has! Tonight's your last night here for four weeks."

"But –"

"Doctor's orders," he said.

"Will you always say that when you want to get your own way?"

"Will I need to?"

"No!" she cried, and pulled his head on to her breast. "I want you, Daniel. So much that I can't find the right words."

"Don't bother with words. There are other ways." Behind them Bella could be heard banging on the door, and he stood up and moved over to it. "I'll show you what I mean later tonight," he said huskily, "and tomorrow night and all the nights after that."

Heart in her eyes, Briony smiled at him. Daniel was hers and life was wonderful.

# The Essie Summers Story

One of the world's most popular and admired authors of romantic fiction, and a special favourite of all Harlequins readers, tells her story.

Essie Summers, the author of such best selling books as "Bride in Flight", "Postscript to Yesterday", "Meet on my Ground" and "The Master of Tawhai" to name just a few, has spent two years bringing the manuscript of her autobiography to its present stage of perfection.

The wit, warmth and wisdom of this fine lady shine, through every page. Her love of family and friends, of New Zealand and Britain, and of life itself is an inspiration throughout the book. Essie Summers captures the essence of a life well lived, and lived to the fullest, in the style of narrative for which she is justly famous.

"The Essie Summers Story", published in paperback, is available at .95 a copy through Harlequin Reader Service, now!